Of Beasts & Common Men

Cameron Stone

To my wife
with love

© 2008 C M Roberts
ISBN 978-0-9561603-0-0

Cameron Stone served in London's Metropolitan Police during the 1970s and 80s. Many events described in this book are true but what remains is not. The author portrays characters and scenes in good faith, altering several to protect their identity.

Of Beasts & Common Men

The Advent

The Dinner Party

A Harvest Supper

The Apprentice

Among Scholars

Of Fate & Sentiment

The Trouble with Pigs

A Higher Learning

An Audience of Trials

The Night of the Icarus

Mists of Blue

Renaissance Ranger

Lambs & Wolves

Pageants & Prejudice

Where Skylarks Sing

Of Beasts & Common Men

Yogi's Smile

A Summer Fete

The Advent

The wound was long, deep and angry. Her forearm spliced, red meat hanging like the heavy jowls of a butcher's dog.

"Steve," she told me. "Steve Coddle." And I scribbled down the name in my police pocket book. "He's my ex. Only he doesn't see it that way. We 'ad a row, he got a knife and..." Her eyes flooded with tears once again. The memory of the recent incident was traumatic for her to recall, but I had to hear her say it. I had to hear the *evidence* that came from her trembling lips before I could act.

"What did he do, Gemma?" I enquired gently, the hospital nurse poised to clean and suture the wound. Domestic violence was all too common, but thankfully, it wasn't every day that I saw a young woman carved open with a kitchen knife, and a sensitive, vulnerable young woman at that. Whether nature or nurture, the unconscious drive to protect was deep-seated in my psyche and anger was beginning to stir inside me. Not a wild frenzied anger - not the stuff she had witnessed. It was a solid, purposeful anger that craved the satisfaction of justice.

"He... he stabbed me," she eventually said, her voice trailing off with emotion and the tears flowed down her pallid cheeks.

The wipers beat an arc against the rain on my windscreen, cold and clammy fingers of rain that clung to the roads, the pavements, the terraced houses, the empty cars parked up in their parallel rows. I turned out my lights and slowly turned a corner in my police car in case he was watching - for surprise was the agent of fortune. And as I turned, as I pulled up a hundred metres or more from the target premises I saw an orange glow in an empty black window; the butt of a cigarette tracing up, then down, then up again. The smoker was nervous. The smoker was expecting me. The smoker was Steve Coddle.

"All units - 53 James Road..." I reported into my personal radio, giving the information in a clear and succinct manner. Coddle had seen me despite my attempt at stealth so there was no point in hanging around. "A hostel... suspect with a knife involved in a serious assault... can I have some back-up please?" And it was with some comfort that I heard the keen and urgent answers from my over worked colleagues, many of whom where abandoning less important assignments to respond to the call of help from one of their own. The police strength of men and women in that heavily populated metropolitan region of Tottenham were only a few, resources already stretched to breaking point.

During the eighties the creation of the Crown Prosecution Service usurped the former police role of prosecuting their ordinary deluge which they did with both success and misgivings. However, the CPS was biased to pursue only those cases that held a high certainty of winning, and so political hegemony skewed the balance of common justice. And as the Government of the day gave extra pay with one hand, they took overtime and rent allowance with the other. The idea of a managerial society and the self-interested individual was everywhere, that paradigm creeping into the Met's old established - even outdated hierarchical institution, and the strain of the job, its violence, and its impotence, its pejorative press, proved too taxing for some. Several brutal riots and a series of damning enquiries concerning police handling had rocked morale which was subterranean. Many colleagues were leaving and those that remained frequently had their backs pressed to the wall.

I didn't wait for back-up to arrive. For me, it was comfort enough to know that some would be on their way. If I could deal with it quickly, I could cancel them and they could return to their usual beck and call. An experienced copper, and well built, it was rare that a situation overwhelmed me, but if it did, then at least my colleagues would be there to pick up the pieces.

The antithesis of the contemporary police stereotype, I was not a bully; I could be compassionate, even empathetic to my public, particularly to victims, yet in adversity I could be formidable too. I rarely carried a truncheon; the wood was so light, like balsa, it was more a hindrance, and anyway I was a wrestler not a hitter, so on passing a skip I selected a few dry cardboard boxes and tore them into strips, rolling them up to pad out my tunic in the hope that it would stave off the first few slashes of a knife attack. Only the first few, because by then I hoped to overpower him – just long enough to control him, extract the knife, and drag him off to acquaint him with Her Majesty's pleasure. This was an era before armoured vests were common place and before armed police became more accessible. It would take several more years and a few more police victims – murdered, and wounded - before anyone took any notice.

Tucking another roll of cardboard into my sleeve, preparing my arm as a knife block, I braced myself at the front door inside the porch way of number 53; rain water spewing from a burst gutter pipe, splattering heavily to the ground like vomit. It was a hostel; a den of thieves. A venue that housed sexual delinquents, villains and deviant characters who enjoyed a transient haven amid life's sordid problems, and many bore their malignant trials as a burden. Alcohol and drugs the paradox that either subdued or fuelled their trauma.

A wiry shrew answered my loud rapport on the door. Only he didn't open it. I was expected. "He's not here!" the landlord insisted behind the door.

"Who?" I enquired, although I knew perfectly well he was lying.

"He's not here!"

"I'm a police officer. Open the door, now!"

I wasn't asking, I had a job to do and I had to do it fast if I was to get my man. It didn't open and I lifted my leg and slammed the heel of my boot *hard* against the door lock. The wood shattered - the door slamming open against its hinges. I was in and the adrenalin was surging thick and fast. I knew where Coddle's room was - the smoker at the window. The shrew cowing back as I emerged, a powerful steam engine dressed in blue and in no mood for fannying about, and the doors of rooms, the staircase and hallway became transformed into a human mass of angry and anxious faces. I pushed past them all as they blocked my way, sending a few onto their backsides as I ploughed a beefy path through those hostile faces.

Coddle's room door was locked, but it gave way easily to my boot and I raised an arm to fend off the blade that might have followed. But it didn't. Coddle wasn't there. It was the group that followed that drew my attention to a neighbouring room; the group that had now gathered to protect it. I sensed their venom. I was thinking on my feet and I had to steal the initiative if I was to survive. Hesitation was the enemy, allowing their retaliation to solidify.

And I felt the warm, wet slime of phlegm in my face as I cleaved a fissure through their tangled limbs of wrath.

Coddle was the first to emerge from the door, and he was the first to throw a punch at me, his fist I blocked with my left arm, his hair I grabbed with my right and I yanked him hard to the floor, he a screaming puppet; hard thumps thudding against my back and shoulders from his cronies behind me, punching and kicking, dislodging my helmet. But I was determined.

"You're nicked!" I snarled, Judges Rules some impracticable process amid the urgent chaos. "Where's the knife?"

Pulling him through that seething morass and in to his room, pushing him into a corner as I quickly searched his cupboards, pulling the bed apart, sending mattress and sheets and covers to the floor; faced with hostility, I didn't have time for courtesy. And the knife, a kitchen knife, the one he had used to slice through his girlfriend's arm, fell to the carpet.

Coddle sprang up and I caught him with my hip, collecting his momentum to sweep him off his feet *ippon sianagi*, a fulcrum throw that landed him against an occasional table. It shattered instantly as I followed him to the ground, wrapping him up like a straightjacket with my arms, squeezing the fetid breath from his rasping lungs until his strength left him. But upon the open floor the blade grinned cold and sharp as a hand picked it up! Gloved in black; wrist cuffed in white.

"Having fun, Stone?" my sergeant enquired.

I awoke with a start. The engine pitch had changed from motorway to ambling rural lane and I glanced at my wife behind the wheel. The sun's rays filtered through the trees overhead, illuminating her face. We had both grown older, yet she was still youthful and pretty, her auburn hair flecked by sunlight. How I loved her, her and the kids, and my eyes traced our children, all four of them asleep in their seats adopting various poses of unconsciousness; mouths open, cheeks flushed and flattened against shoulders, saliva threads like sinuous stalactites descending to damp, dark pools of cotton.

It was going to be a big change for them, I knew. Indeed, it was going to be a big change for us all. But despite the uncertainty of our future, here among Devon's pleasant rolling hills, the insecurity of the unknown offered a better opportunity, a better life. Even at its most belligerent, rural life would not equal the certainty of high crime, high costs, and high material expectations that is London's lot.

I had retired from the police. I had left it all behind. I knew I would have to change, indeed, I wanted to change. In London's malicious face, cynicism, aggression and a loss of faith in humanity had tainted my good nature, a quality of character I was eager to restore. How or whether such a transformation would occur, however, I had no idea. We had no plan, just a belief that what we were doing was right for us, taking on this new life with a brave and passionate heart; my wife by my side, unwavering in her love and support.

This is a story about our new life in Dartmoor. A life that now seems far removed from England's south east conurbation. It is a powerful story, but one of fun, wonder, adventure and trial, as seen through my eyes, the eyes of Cameron Stone; a former London policeman haunted by poignant memories.

The Dinner Party

I surrendered a bottle of Bordeaux to our host and we were ushered into a world of warmth and comfort; rich carpets lapping against lime washed walls that were laden with oil paintings in garnished frames. Ceilings beamed with the smile of an ancient oak whilst an elderly retriever inspected us. Snorting dispassionately from the crotch of my trousers, he regarded us with glazed, rabbit burrow eyes.

The lounge was busy with guests, engrossed in glib social chit-chat; log fire crackling from the hearth, subdued lights, upholstered chairs that could comfortably sink a battleship. The battleship, however, had long been decommissioned, rising stiffly to introduce himself, standing erect, shoulders back, chest out; I imagined him balancing a sea log upon his balding pate. A direct old gentleman, steely grey eyes, small nose and mouth, Captain Claret extend a formal handshake.

"And you are?"

"Stone," I told him, "Cameron Stone, and this is my wife, Lucy."

He introduced us to a woman some fifteen years his junior; high cheekbones, swarthy complexion, large bust, narrow waist. "She's not my wife," he boasted, ostensibly guarding his mouth with his hand. "Horsy sort of people are you?" he ventured, eyeing us suspiciously, sipping from his single malt tumbler.

"No," I rallied, suppressing a smile. "We're more doggy and chicky sort of people."

Eyebrows were primed, their conversation skewered, the stiffening smiles of guests were concealed behind raised sherry glasses.

"Er .. nuts anyone?" Our hosts were a generous and sincere couple, nobly extending an invitation to Lucy and me to wine and dine us at their home. It was an opportunity to get to know some local characters; these locals, however, were not the stereotypes we expected. Well-heeled and eloquent, many had retired to this piece of Devon for peace and quiet, and who could blame them?

Another couple introduced themselves, "...and, yes, we are married."

"So are we," Lucy told them *sotto voce*. "But don't tell anyone."

"So how many do you have?" they enquired.

"I can only afford the one husband, I'm afraid."

"No, I mean dogs and chickens. How many do you have?"

I concentrated my mind into a mental calculus.

"Two dogs, twelve chickens ..."

"Oh, we're down to six. The fox got the others," she stated.

"... two geese, four guinea pigs, two cats, five doves ..." I hesitated, something was missing.

"And a peahen," Lucy reminded me.

"Good heavens," the husband declared. "You have got your hands full."

"And four kids."

"Goats as well?"

"No - children. The noisy, eat you out of house and home type." They were stunned with silence, scenes of mayhem and discord infecting their minds. 'Why?' was a question unasked. "Didn't have a TV for the first few years," I offered lamely. "Do you have any?"

"Yes," the wife managed to answer, a little bemused. "One in the lounge and another in the bed ..."

"Sorry," I grinned. "I meant children. Do you have any?"

"God, no!" she blurted. "But where are they?" And she looked anxiously around Lucy's skirt as if the horrid little things might pop out from beneath the hem at any moment.

"At home," Lucy told her, and the wife virtually collapsed with relief. "Some friends are babysitting."

"How lovely." Our distinguished host and cook, hands still damp, had emerged from the kitchen. "How old are they?" My mental calculus at work once again.

"Eight, nine, 11 and 12," Lucy told her. Women are always better at that sort of thing; God forbid anyone should ask me their dates of birth.

"Big babies!"

"Three boys and a girl, the girl is number two."

"Our youngest son was supposed to be a girl," I explained. "But it didn't quite work out that way."

"It never does," she agreed, the childless couple slinking away. "So, what brings you to this corner of Devon?"

"I'm retired," I told her. The babble of conversation had subdued as ears strained to listen.

"What did you do?"

"Oh, I was a policeman," I tried to announce with indifference, "in London."

Like some huge distended bubble, the revelation bounced among the heads of the astonished audience before rising up to the rafters where it burst against the candelabra.

"Ha! Policeman you say?" the Captain guffawed loudly. "My God, I knew he was on to us the moment I set eyes on him! Got that tax disc renewed yet, Arthur?"

Arthur said nothing; a portly chap across the room, blowing his nose with a handkerchief; a nose so heavily veined it could have been mistaken for a map of a metropolitan water system.

Like the electrician whose brains they want to pick on the fineries of DIY home wiring, or the medical doctor plugged for all the ails their audience might possess, I appreciated their indifference to my former profession. Their polite ignorance, their avoidance of tedious questions that can spoil many a social evening, we were spared of that and I was grateful. However, spared though we were, we knew precious little of the preparations for the next summer fete, the perfect golf swing, or the German U-boats that plagued the British Fleet. So out of boredom and ennui the ghost of winter began to haunt my mind ... wandering, drifting back to an incident some ten years earlier...

"Cameron?" my police inspector informed me. "Get yourself a quick cup of tea, then report to DI Taylor, upstairs. The Serious Crime Squad wants you for a job."

I held a healthy regard for many CID squads, although perhaps a little less for some of the more spurious types that operated from New Scotland Yard. But I couldn't disguise my surprise that early morning, my fingers and toes still numb with frost as I struggled out of my motorbike cladding, warming myself gratefully against a radiator in the station canteen.

Normally abandoned at such an ungodly hour, I entered the CID office clutching my polystyrene cup of hot, sweet tea, where I met my colleague, Paul and a formidable gang of plainclothes heavyweights; some standing, some seated, one perched casually against an adjacent desk. "PC Stone, I presume?"

"That's me."

Their probing eyes quickly assessing this 'woodentop'; this young, stocky uniformed officer summoned to assist them. And I assessed them - a cagey, furtive bunch of hard noses; had I not known better, I could easily have mistaken them for night-club bouncers.

"We need you two for your firearms skills, just as backup for a job this morning. One James Keith Bane is due to collect some money from his solicitor this morning. Knowing his reputation, his brief wisely decided to grass him up." He paused to light a cigarette, eyes squinting from the smoke. "Bane likes Jags and Daimlers, and has been known to use disguises. We want him for three counts of armed robbery, unlawful wounding, and GBH on one of our traffic colleagues ..." he hesitated, wearing a pained expression on his features, blue smoke billowing in torrents with each uttered syllable. "Silly bastard tried to stop him, and got run over for his pains. He's a right nasty animal, to put a finer point on it."

"So, where would you like us?" I asked, expecting him to offer some sensible strategy.

"If we need you," he went on, deliberating on an adjacent wall map that was densely swathed in coloured flag pins, each representing a local crime statistic. "You can go here, and here."

I looked at Paul. He looked at me. It was immediately clear that DI Taylor had little or no experience of firearms. He had positioned us directly opposite each other.

"I don't think that's a good idea, guv," Paul told him tactfully. "Perhaps we could have a quick recce first?"

The observation point was a disused building, a window on the first floor providing a good view of the solicitor's office nearby; a broad pavement extending from a line of terraced houses to a busy road - a potential nightmare for the public if the bullets started flying. But as I was well aware, circumstances such as these were often far from ideal. "Let's hope he comes early," I muttered to myself, watching through the binoculars, "before the traffic builds up."

Whether it was by magic or simple coincidence, a Daimler happened to pull up outside; a woman driving and a man alighting from the passenger door; tall, medium build, silver hair. Nothing like the photos the detectives were examining.

"Nope," one decided, tossing the images aside. But the woman leaving the car caught my eye; her face was among the handful of photographs that covered the table beside me.

"That's his wife!" I declared. DI Taylor quickly picked it up to compare, watching them both crossing the pavement and enter through the solicitor's front door.

"Jesus, it's him," he confirmed. "GO! GO! GO!"

No time to form some plan - no time to discuss the finer points of detail. Now was the time to do the job and do it cleanly, there were no prizes for coming second. The adrenaline began to ooze as I descended the steps in short, jerky movements, my grip tightening on the butt of my .38 Smith and Wesson revolver, still holstered, still concealed beneath my coat.

The rules of engagement were very strict; the legacy of too many mistakes. Too many police 'cowboys' had dented public confidence. Too many victims had suffered. Too many families harboured resentment and bitterness, for they were also victims, although perhaps many were ignorant of the responsibility and the danger, real and potential, many policemen had to face each working day.

"There are times when policemen do not deserve their pay packets," one retiring sage once told me. "And there are times when they deserve more, more than anyone will ever know."

He wasn't wrong.

"MOVE - NOW!" Normally mild and easygoing, my uniformed colleague had been transformed into an aggressive, no-nonsense individual with a purpose, a mission. I rarely saw this side of him; he had served as a soldier in Northern Ireland, an experience I had never addressed, but the danger of the situation had infected both of us. He, snarling at pedestrians and passing car drivers that were oblivious to the imminent peril that threatened them as we raced towards the building line. Me, dodging among the parked vehicles, edging closer towards the target's car.

The Sweeney types were there, excellent as part of the street furniture; a couple chatting on the pavement - perhaps good mates just passing by, another leaning against a wall. Then the front door opened and Bane's wife was the first to emerge.

Wait! I told myself. Wait until he's left the building, I don't want him running back inside; a hostage incident was the last thing we wanted to deal with. Take him when he's clear.

Bane emerged unaware of the ambush we were about to spring. His wife opening the car and he, ten paces behind her, a good distance from the solicitor's door. Then he saw me, his face collapsing, a picture of surprise and confusion; sliding his hand inside his jacket as I knelt behind my revolver, taking aim.

"Armed Police!"

But his feet didn't touch the floor. Grabbed with such ferocity, members of the Squad literally lifted him - wholesale – and rammed him into the pavement.

Bane now a ragged, pathetic doll.

But it was the movement I noticed from the corner of my eye; Bane's wife turning from the car – and I was up and sprinting - shouldering her. She, squealing with fright as I pinned her against the bodywork lest she should threaten them. Lest she too carried a firearm ...

"Are you a golfer?" Mrs Bane suddenly enquired.

"Sorry?"

"Golf?" holding her fork in both hands, about to strike a strawberry from her Pavlova, and her feminine hands dissolved into rough, stumpy fingers. They belonged to Captain Claret at the dining table, demonstrating his swing.

"No," I answered, shaking the residue of fatigue from my memory.

"Thought all policemen played golf," he grumbled, stuffing meringue into his mouth. "Rugby then? You've got the build for it."

I shook my head. "My school didn't do it, so I missed out I'm afraid."

"Thought all schools did rugby," he complained. "Did in my day."

"Judo," I ventured. "Wrestling. Tug of war." But these things were foreign to him. "Hill walking."

"*Hill walking!*" he exploded in an enfilade of meringue. "Sounds like golf to me!"

Drizzlewick was a surprisingly large village. Surprising because if you travelled by car you would notice only a handful of houses, a pub, a shop and perhaps a church; the rest concealed among intimate lanes and tortuous tracks that lead to nowhere in particular. Nowhere, that is, unless you were on horseback, or on foot enjoying the wooded hills and vales, their verdant leaves glazed by a damp and earthy air and blessed by sunkissed pools of light.

Springs would gurgle cheerfully from granite banks, weaving their fluid paths among the roots of ash and alder, and gushing to the swollen river, freshly stained by umber peat. By later frosts the denuded limbs would pale to the embroidery of lichens, laced with holly, ivy and viridian moss, and veiled by the gossamer webs of a winter mist.

I had no connection with Dartmoor, no primeval instinct with which to draw me to its boggy roots, save that it reminded me of my infant past, perhaps an imprint of my youth and exiled identity with the North Yorkshire Moors. Yet here we were, nestling against nature's breast, embraced by sessile oaks and tawny heaths, brackish streams and heather nods, while salient tors like crone's teeth did chafe and tear the wild and pewter skies.

A Harvest Supper

He regarded us with a squint, a glass eye fixed somewhere at Lucy's left breast while his good one roved independently – although sometimes it seemed the other way around. "Do you have tickets?" He was one of the village ancients, one of a declining nucleus of retired parochials who had dominated Drizzlewick's parish society for years.

"No, but we can pay." I offered him some cash.

"Local, are you?"

"Tanglewood," I told him and he cocked a twitching eyebrow; some frenzied hawk moth pupae. "In the valley."

"I know where it is," he growled. "So you must be the new incomers."

"That's right," and I introduced our gang, Drizzlewick's answer to the Von Trap family, all wearing their Sunday best.

"Well, you need tickets," he insisted, "can't come without tickets."

"We've brought our own supper," Lucy explained, showing him our bread rolls and salad as evidence. "Hyacinth thought it would be alright."

"Bah, she's no business thinkin' anything," he complained, then stabbed his thumb towards the door, a gesture of grudging acceptance. The mention of a name had done the trick.

"I think we've just been positively vetted," I whispered in Lucy's ear.

"I doubt it's as easy as that," she answered, and we entered with scepticism, bracing ourselves for the next acerbic.

The parish hall was a modest size, perhaps large enough to accommodate some forty people seated comfortably before the stage. The stage itself bore two tables and five chairs, the chairs containing a variety of zoophytic specimens that were Drizzlewick's venerables; the Reverend Keel, Miss Pinch, Colonel Brazier, and Captain Claret.

One chair was vacant, however, and remained so until all parishioners who were coming had come; the tables occupied, the cold meals, still entombed by cling-film, a tenant at each place. And the Cyclops, as we unkindly nicknamed him, had left his sentry post to enter stage left, taking residence in the fifth chair, his glass eye roaming Miss Pinch's ample frame.

Armed with a dessert spoon, Captain Claret stood up to bang with authority on the table to hush the attending audience. Not that there was any need, we were all quiet, stunned into subservience; the crowd consisting of families with children whose ages ranged from babes to 12 year olds – their wiser, elder siblings escaping this annual ritual that was Drizzlewick's Harvest Supper, a celebration of the Parish's achievements.

The Captain cleared his throat, a Jutland duel between phlegm and trachea.

"Welcome to Drizzlewick's Harvest Supper," he finally announced. "Before we begin this excellent supper, prepared by the Colonel's wife," picking a nail, the Colonel cast his eyes downward, a modest composure, his portly build giving proud acclaim to such a comestible wedlock, "we should bow our heads for Grace."

Dutifully, we bowed our heads as the Reverend arose to bless the ceremony. A kindly chap who appeared as a large, bear-like character, his cherub face and nose partially eclipsed by a beard that resembled a thicket of blackthorn.

"Lord, bless this harvest of bread and meat, bless the food we are about to eat, bless the children one and all, and bless the rest that attend this hall. Amen."

"E's on form today," complimented a woman from an adjacent table, revealing a vacant front tooth amid an alignment of crapulent monoliths.

The Reverend loved poetry. His sermons, staid and typically ecclesiastic to begin with, would often conclude in some sort of rhyming prose. Sometimes it would rhyme, however, and sometimes it would not, a challenge for those parishioners who indulged in the sport of guessing his final verse.

We ate our salad and drank our squash and wine as heads turned and tongues wagged, glancing with curiosity as they devoured their suppers.

"What are they staring at?" said Edward indignantly.

"They're just curious," I tried to suggest.

"Rude if you ask me," declared Anna.

"Imagine how zoo animals must feel," David empathised, John placing a finger up his nostril as a means of audience entertainment, until Lucy pulled away his offending hand. Then he suddenly erupted into laughter.

At a neighbouring table one farmer had buried a stout digit into his extended proboscis. John replied in kind, and stuck out his tongue to compliment the gesture. The farce repeated by the same, his leather face gaping with mirth.

"At least they're friendly," Lucy sighed.

Once bellies had been sated, their torpid conversations were subdued by one simple action; the Captain scraping back his chair upon the stage. He cleared his throat, and arising, thumped the silverware once again against the table.

"The Agenda will include comments from the Cricket Secretary," the audience applauded like damp seals. "The Bridge Committee..."

More applause.

"The Summer Fete..."

Same.

"The Women's Institute..."

With more than a little feminine enthusiasm – less from the men.

"Concluding with the swaling arrangements for the coming months."

We clapped dynamically, as we had done throughout, only this time, to our chagrin our applause was met with silence. We hadn't the faintest idea what swaling was (heather burning), but it seemed like a good idea to applaud at the time while everyone, hither to, had appeared to be in such a supportive mood. But our clapping soon receded, crushed beneath their hostile gaze.

The Captain sat down, cleared his throat once again then stood up as if he were hoisting the flag; stomach in - chest out. With a cravat serving as a Shakespearean ruff beneath his chin, he reminded me of an orator about to launch into Hamlet. "As Secretary of the Drizzlewick Cricket Club I'd just like to say we've had a splendid season this year... absolutely splendid, and well done to all who sailed in her."

Everyone applauded again, except us - *once bitten.* The Captain sat, cleared his throat then stood up again.

"I'd like to introduce Colonel Brazier."

The Captain finally docked in his chair as the Colonel, wrestling his corpulent frame from his seat, stood proud like his stomach. "Yes, thank you Captain Claret," the Colonel effused. Then he would twitch and jerk his head, exclaiming "*What?*" An enquiring glance to who ever was unfortunate enough to be at his side, an anxious moment for the unwary, but Miss Pinch was not the sort to be easily ruffled.

"Bridge," Miss Pinch reminded him, accustomed to his idiosyncratic ways.

"Bridge?" he snorted. "Excellent, well done! Absolutely splendid! Nothing more to add." And with that he deposited himself upon his plinth behind the table.

The chair scraped beside him. The Captain cleared his throat and hoisted his sails. "Thank you, Colonel," he said. "Nothing more to add," he agreed.

Then, positioning his stern above his chair, the Captain dropped anchor.

For a moment or two, nothing happened. It was as if the Captain's workings had a delaying mechanism until the seat slid back again, the cough, the cranking of the spine, the military bristle. "I believe it's your turn, William," he half introduced, a little fazed by the informality of William's non-military status.

Captain Claret retired to his chair as William stood up, leaning heavily on the table with his fists as he did so. William was the 'Cyclops' whom we had unkindly dubbed, his glass eye torn from breast *de* Pinch to rove the front of the ensemble, prompting a rash of feminine self-consciousness. Cleavages were hastily concealed, their cardigans drawn like drapes, folding arms defensively as others embraced their companion for protection from this itinerant voyeur. The Colonel's wife, however, ever accustomed to self-sacrifice, braced her upholstery for the object *de* distraction, his pupil alighting like some bluebottle fly.

"The Summer Fete," he announced. "A good show, well attended despite the damn awful weather... Excellent result with Mrs Brown's jam... Shame about the tombola…"

"Hear, hear," said the Captain.

"Hear, hear," said the Reverend Keel.

The Colonel, however, simply twitched and jerked his head. *"What?"* he fired.

"Tom-bola," explained Miss Pinch pointedly.

"Never heard of 'im," growled the Colonel.

Their performance could have been amusing had they all been less serious. As it was, they wore their duty like an overripe loincloth, threadbare with ritual abuse, stale with bucolic repetition.

I glanced at the long-suffering attendants as they watched. Even their children appeared equally subdued. Perhaps rare in some urban neighbourhoods, such distinctive rural cultures were often a fusion of middle and lower-classes, a community in harmony with their traditions and social graces.

There were the hill farmers, yet only a few affluent incomers among them could afford to play at it as other impoverished neighbours scraped a living from the soil. There were the farm hands, deplete in every kind of wealth or possessions, who enjoyed their labours despite so little prospect. Then there was perhaps a builder, a plumber and an electrician or two. Some were indigenous and some had joined the party, as we had, later in life.

There were the semi-retired professionals; the restaurant owner, the accountant, the shopkeeper and the publican. Then last of all, there were the retired middle-class misfits: Captain Claret, William the former Civil Servant, and Colonel Brazier. And then, of course, there was Miss Pinch.

A former schoolmistress from Clacton-on-Sea, Hilary Pinch was a spinster, an austere sort who simply loathed children. Her early inheritance from a wealthy late relative had provided her with a comfortable home, a paddock and stable. But it was Miss Pinch's passion for horses and fox hunting that had bought her some reprieve among the Drizzlewick community. It was also her passion for playing the piano.

"…and the sum of forty seven pounds and 82 pence was raised at the WI's Shove-a-penny night in aid of charity," she read out, pausing briefly to inspect us above jet-rimmed glasses.

We applauded, as we must.

Her lenses were so thick they made her eyes appear twice their normal size and as she blinked her giant lashes meshed like drosera flytrap. "And now it is time to entertain the *children.*" The word was repugnant to her, and as she prised her tongue from her palate, you could almost touch the audience's muted groan of anticipation.

Miss Pinch left the stage to descend upon a corner of the hall, children flinching as she approached - relieved as she passed them by. Then on adjusting the piano seat, she licked a fingertip and applied it to the score sheet. Miss Pinch finally settled her sinews and began, the ivory segments compelled to jump with vigorous forte.

"Oranges and lemons from the bells of Saint Clements…" she sang with gusto, her sickle-like glances swiping at the heads of the disconsolate congregation as we trailed behind, our mouths opening and closing as lizards gaping on a warm, balmy day. Older children slugged with boredom, their drooping skulls propped by languid arms while the little ones hid beneath the tables.

I looked longingly at the exit door, too far to make a run for it without drawing unwelcome attention, and it took a great deal of willpower to suppress the urge to climb out of the adjacent window. But as each verse took hypnotic control, I began to yawn, my hand attempting to conceal my apathy. My eyes growing tired as I fought to concentrate...

My first nightshift was something of a trial. Sure, I was accustomed to the occasional late night, even the odd early morning, but night duty had its own nuances. For a start, the night dragged on well past the hour of three. Prior to that, the city was alive with night revellers, with traffic slipping in and then out of the metropolis as they ferried their cargo of drinkers, socialites and entertainment seekers. But by three, the streets usually began to settle down as the last dregs of the evening melted towards their bed... or someone else's.

Sometimes, cars were broken into, stolen by those who had missed the night bus or the final tube home. Sometimes, domestic fights would flare up as the inebriated practiced old habits, opening those wounds of old. But sometimes it was quiet. Quiet enough to amble the weary night, tread softly along alleyways, and loiter among doorways deep and dark to watch the unwary, the odd taxi dropping off his final fare. The odd vagrant scouring the gutters for half a fag, and the gentle chinking of milk bottles as the milk man went about his early chores.

I was tired. My young eyes were heavy with fatigue, and my aching feet walked under protest, desperate to rest. I stopped briefly at a road junction and watched hypnotically as the lights changed from red, to amber, to green. My mind was a haze of exhaustion and as I turned a corner, one of dozens I had negotiated that first night, the warm scent of dough rocked me on my heels. A baker had fired up his ovens and was making bread. It took all my self-discipline to avoid his shop step which seemed intoxicatingly seductive as a place to nap. I passed by, groggy with stupor as the early morning tide of traffic began to build.

In that early rush hour, as a string of vehicles yielded to the ruby gaze of a traffic light, their drivers witnessed a young police constable colliding against every single parking metre along Tottenham Court Road.

Someone smiling caught my eye, an incongruous display of pleasure. It was another family seated at the table behind us and the father leaned forward, beside my ear. "I think you're very brave to come," he told me. "I know how you must be feeling," he empathised, "we felt exactly the same as you when we first came here."

"And you came again?" I replied in disbelief and he grinned.

"You have to accept they're just a bunch of old farts who need to feel important," he explained. "They once had pretty high-powered jobs and they hate being redundant. They're too wrapped up in themselves and their parish council meetings to care about anything else." I raised an eyebrow, a ripple of concern. "Oh, cummon," my confidant encouraged, "give them a bit of slack. They're not so bad on their own, they just look frightening when they're together. This performance is just a front. It's all complete bollocks."

"I agree with you," I told him. "How long have you been in Drizzlewick?" He didn't sound local.

"We moved here from Oxford three years ago. There are a few more recent incomers in the village, too, but they didn't come to the Supper." Indeed, we too were beginning to wish we had stayed at home.

"I'm Tony," he offered me his hand.

"Cameron," I returned, "we're down at Tanglewood."

"You're the retired policeman, I gather."

"Gossip runs fast here," I said, a little peeved to learn we had become common knowledge.

"They're rather like children," Tony explained. "They like to know where they stand. I'm the antique dealer by the way," he grinned, "more an antique than a dealer some would say."

I had found an ally, a friend whose philosophy would prove invaluable in the years ahead. Years that would test and stretch my urban mind, and ease the veil of ignorance that shaded me from the erudite of life.

"Thank you one and all," the Reverend Keel had stood to deliver his parting speech, and as we watched and listened I noticed several were following his every word, their mouths miming every syllable and rhyme:

"Thank you for coming to this Harvest Supper,

With apple tart and bread and butter.

To celebrate this day of blessing,

Let us thank the Lord, the Lamb and King,

And praise the parish… with…."

Money was exchanged beneath tables, and bets were whispered into ears as the vicar floundered, distracted by those who silently mouthed 'hymn' and others, with odds against, mouthing something very different.

"With... with some words."

"Bugger!" someone cursed, losing his or her bet.

"He's stuffed it again," another lamented. The sentence drowned by weary piano wire as Miss Pinch croaked a traditional hymn.

"All things bright and beautiful, all creatures great and small..."

The Apprentice

"Bells are up, an' sally's away," it was announced and each bell ringer would pull systematically with a slow, steady heave on the sally, the rope's fluffy handgrip. From high above us the bells would tumble from their wooden stays, a cacophony of hammers knocking against their vibrant walls as the metalled casts clashed like discordant town criers for all to hear in Drizzlewick.

Inside, the beams would groan, the ropes creaking like ships moored in the night, the tower swaying by the inertia as a drunken matelot's sigh. Each man and woman was locked in concentration, their faces creased by effort, stretching and pulling in rhythm. "Four five!" the tower captain would call out the changes, ringers adjusting their pull to follow their number. "Five four!" The bells singing out, peeling in musical forte.

It was a science new to the likes of me and I would stand in the cloistered corner of the church tower, marvelling at their performance while nursing the blisters that had erupted from my amateurish attempts. These stalwarts made the event look simple, but to a newcomer the practise was far from easy.

"It takes about two year to learn the ropes," George warned me, pink faced and wheezing beneath a bristle moustache; like a badger grunting at a florid sun.

"It took me long enough," Hyacinth admitted coyly. A kind and honest sort her, only affliction was her looks, battered and hoary from years of tending sheep on the moor; tall with grey steel hair, she possessed a hooked nose and chin hair that resembled a crag ascending a tangle of silver birch.

"So what brings a London policeman to Drizzlewick then?"

George ventured, relieved to snatch a few minutes rest.

"No reason, really," I admitted, "other than a love for the moor. It's a great place to bring up children."

They all nodded in agreement for a moment, satisfied with my explanation. But I knew, behind the ostensible mask of politeness, these latest incomers would be subject to much scrutiny. People were friendly here, certainly friendlier than they were in London, and not just in Drizzlewick, in local towns too. Londoners, however, perhaps more familiar with change and to inquiline cultures, were generally more tolerant of visitors both from home and abroad. The Devon suspicion of outsiders it seemed was founded on insecurity; a barrier of reservation they bound with the barbed wire attitudes of rural conservatism.

This was my reason for taking up bell ringing, to get to know the true locals who had been here for generations, to dissolve inhibitions and forge new friendships. But like the granite land they were born to, they sometimes proved to be remote and impervious characters. Indeed, I soon realised that it was going take much more than a weekly visit to the belfry to win their confidence.

"You've got to 'ave been dead an' buried for thirty year or more avore you're accepted as local," Hyacinth once told me.

"How long have you lived here?" I enquired, enjoying the brief respite. The bells were up, perched high on their wooden stays.

"Fifty seven year," she told me proudly.

"Bah," Arthur complained. Threadbare and torn, his cardigan resembled the sloughed velvet skin of some rutting stag. "You're just a vurriner."

Hyacinth glared at him.

"Widcum," she corrected rather haughtily. "An' you're a Tavi man, an' tha's much longer."

"My father brought me 'ere when I was just a biy avore the war," he rallied.

"Which war then?" George baited him. "Napoleon?"

"You scoff," Arthur growled," he were at the Somme."

"Bloody long ways from here!" George chuckled.

Arthur said nothing. He lacked the sharp wit of his contemporaries, but was wise enough to know it.

It took some time for me to understand their dialect. Indeed, some expressions were far beyond my comprehension and guessing was very much a lottery. Few of the indigenous population were left, however, and much of the original old Devon idioms had since been diluted. A number of political catalysts that had caused younger generations to move elsewhere and seek alternative careers had impoverished many of the farms, predominantly the sheep and beef industries of upland areas. The communities dissolved by incomers – vurriners, *foreigners* such as I.

"So what does tha plan to do with th'self, young man?" Arthur enquired.

"I don't really know," I admitted. "But now I'm in the countryside, I suppose I ought to learn how to look after it."

That first winter proved to be a bitterly cold experience. Our run down home, remote and peaceful, possessed an electric immersion for hot water, a handful of impotent electric storage heaters, an ancient iron stove and rotting casement windows that bled rainwater and wind, their curtains billowing and sighing with every gasp.

By day we kept warm by cutting up timber, the children sent off in sorties to collect wood while Lucy and I tried in vain to keep the stove alight. Then at night we would sit huddled together on the sofa, our legs tucked beneath us to conserve body heat, our hands concealed within the depths of our multi-layered bodies, our faces masked by scarves and knitted hats. Only our smarting eyes were visible, our breath vapour competing with the wood smoke that trickled from the stove's decrepit seams.

Then one February morning the taps suddenly ran dry, the water pipes belching and gurgling with protest, the intake frozen by a freak Baltic wind that had hardened the ground surface; now cracked and fissured by winter's bite. It reminded me of another adventure, at another time, in another place...

"Frrsk brrnm!"

"Dltrmnb lwng!" Our words, the few we exchanged, were snatched from our mouths by the wind as it howled, cold and penetrating.

Bloated with insulation, our orange forms appeared alien against the winter snow. Dark and bleak against the skyline, this mountain wall had become a malevolent place. Each of us was burdened with a rucksack, and we were burdened too with anxious thoughts as the blizzard filled every crevice in our coats; every pleat and every crease; our eyelashes clotted by ice.

"I'm too cold!" someone complained, and he slumped to his knees, the snow deep and enveloping. Our predicament was growing worse. "I'm just going to sit here and die!" But he was kicked, hard, up the backside.

"Get up! Get up!"

We were all exhausted, our stamina sapped by the bitter gale that had savaged this godforsaken rock. We had stumbled in circles, an orange train of torpid souls. Our strength taxed by Boreas' wrath. Nature's crippling breath eroding our resolve as we trudged blindly, toiling through the heavy snow; the hail unmerciful, our features stung and raw.

"There's supposed to be a pond here!" our leader yelled plaintively, wiping the laminate map with his coat sleeve.

"Probably iced over and filled with snow!" I yelled back.

There were six of us; one group of several police cadets that were enduring a winter exercise in North Wales. We had been given a map reference to an isolated barn, and it lay in an alluvial valley beyond this steep mountain saddle of Glyda Faw. Exposed to the savage elements, the route ahead looked perilous, but we knew we had to get off that mountain if we were to survive at all.

"Wait here!" I told them. "I'm going to see if there's a way down!"

"Don't take any risks!" our leader warned.

"I don't intend to!" I replied with a grin, adjusting my straps, clapping my frozen gloves in an explosion of powder crystals.

Gingerly I approached the edge, a white apron tongue that descended into the valley depths that were dark and mysterious. Some twenty metres I carefully traversed, testing the surface, my eyes trawling the descent for signs of danger, but I could see none.

Another twenty metres and the storm had subdued, sheltered from the assailing blizzard above. Then I slipped, thumping onto my backside, and skated off down the slope in mild panic before I managed to stop abruptly, slamming my heels as brakes into that crisp snow mantle. Then laughing with relief I turned to hail the others, and found them following; a handful of terra cotta figures, glissading behind me. And together we rode that mountainside, whooping and hooting with exhilaration.

We climbed Snowdon the next day, enjoying a tranquil December air. Cirrus clouds dancing vividly in a clear vault sky, both sun and moon exalted; a flaxen orb mocked by a jaunty lunar grin. Snowdon's lofty terrace some squeaking carpet of alabaster beneath our tread as we passed spangled cairns of frost to the summit. We beheld a panorama of somnolent giant heads, their craggy brows encased in hoods of snow, while icy threads like veins of gold glittered from the valleys far below.

At Tanglewood, our water pipe traversed adjacent fields and hedgerows, winding a subterranean path among igneous boulders that heralded the air like a clutch of petrified beasts. Concealed by brambles and copper bracken, the exposed pipe lay in a hollow, remaining solid and unyielding despite a bonfire, a hair-drier, and a train of hot water bottles.

For two weeks the freeze lasted; fourteen days of bathing at a neighbour's house, a quarter of a mile or so away, using their washing machine, transporting bucket loads of water to refill our toilet cistern - which we flushed once a day, and water to drink and cook our food. It was a grim event; the ordeal softened only by the knowledge of other poor wretches throughout the world who lived in much greater squalor. Despite the chores, despite the cold and the ramshackle facilities, we knew we lived like kings in our tranquil estate.

When the thaw finally arrived, we applauded and danced to the rhythm of water that gasped, sighed and finally coughed from the taps in an extravagant gush.

It had been a valuable lesson; an education to the essentials of rural living, and a siege mentality soon prevailed. Like inured veterans we began lagging pipes, stockpiling preserves and fuel, even accumulating salt grit in preparation for another hard freeze. We couldn't afford to be benighted again, discarding the soft blanket of dependency that we formerly adopted in London; spoilt by the commercial demand for civilised trappings. Indeed, living in Dartmoor was more than a way of life. Its fortification against the elements was as much a part of its cultural identity as its anathema to urban attitudes.

When Spring finally arrived we were privy to its subtle awakening. Like drops of milky dew the gentle hoods of *nivalis* would herald the nubile air, blackthorn, larch then a chestnut horse would be among the first to unfurl its verdant fingers to the sky while narcissus trumpets acclaimed the woodland floor beneath. It was a magical scene, our home a hide as we watched nature's cloth unfold.

"I saw some deer," David announced one early morning as they waited for the school bus. Lucy burdened with John's school bag as John dawdled just behind. "Five of them drinking by the river. I was so close to them, but they legged it when they saw me."

"I saw a badger yesterday," said Anna, not wishing to be outdone by her elder brother, tying back her hair for perhaps the fourth time that morning. Some evenings I would see the badger, like a diminutive bear, my car headlights illuminating his lolloping gait as he foraged for molluscs and insects.

"And I saw an elephant," said Edward, as they boarded the bus, "…in a zoo." His school bag was so large he reminded me of a hermit crab occupying a size 12 boot.

Our feral garden, infested by agrostis and fescue grasses, had bloomed in a rash of pink swathes of campion and foxglove. The outstretched limbs of buzzards sailed high above - the pair crying out as they spiralled high into the azure.

"I want to study for a diploma in Countryside Management," I told him. The tutor slightly fazed by this mature student to be. We were roughly the same age, an incongruous sight among the spotty school leavers that thronged the reception hall, their parents in tow.

"W... why?" he stammered. "I mean, sure, but what qualifications do you have?"

"Hardly any," I admitted.

"What background do you have? We only do full-time courses."

"Police," I whispered, as if selling contraband.

He hesitated a moment and I braced myself for a stab of prejudice – perhaps a driving altercation or some past grudge against the law. But my fears were unfounded.

"W... well," he continued, collecting himself, squeezing the contours of his briefcase.

"Can you write?"

"Crime reports, statements, that sort of thing. Policemen do little else these days," I smiled weakly, slightly irked by his ignorance. I was slow to realise that outside the Force, few people appreciate what police men and women actually do; the plethora of television dramas perhaps a testament to the public's fascination. "Oh, and I once wrote a novel," I added for good measure, "about eighty thousand words, but it wasn't published."

It was a gamble. To admit to writing anything longer than an academic essay was like admitting to insanity. I was among the thousands of literary hopefuls that had trod the very same path of submissions and had endured the many letters of rejection. Indeed, few had even bothered to read them – the publishing system so inept.

Sitting back in his chair, the tutor allowed himself a smile.

"Well, Mr Stone," he concluded, "I think you should do very well."

Among Scholars

That first day of term I found myself among the company of young people; hundreds thronging the entrance steps, the corridors, and the student lounge. Within minutes I fended off such questions as, "Can you tell me how to get to the Agriculture First Years?" or "Is this the right way for Equine Husbandry?" They had mistaken me for a tutor and I had to explain to them that I too was a new student, and just as lost as they, although few seemed convinced. One girl, barely sixteen, came rushing up to me, ruddy faced and close to tears. "I can't find my Admission card," she reported, and I consoled her, calmly directing her to the reception office – about the only location I knew.

On discovering my classroom I hesitated outside the door, surveying the young faces through the door's narrow window. What would I talk to them about? Could I relate to them? Sure, I was young once, but I was less certain they could relate to me.

"Assessing the enemy?"

He was a tallish chap, perhaps a year or two younger than I with tanned face and receding hairline that had been bleached by the sun.

"Yes, yes I suppose I am," I admitted, delighted to find another mature student. At last, someone I could relate to, someone with whom we might share something, a casual subject perhaps, such as *life*. "I never thought I'd get here," I told him.

"Nor me, I've been away these past few months," he explained. "Cut it a bit fine, only arrived an hour ago. So what's your forte?"

"Sorry?"

"Your speciality? Mine's ecology, for my sins,"

"Oh, nothing quite so impressive," I said, "just a healthy regard for nature …"

"I like a moment to size them up too," he said sharing the opportunity to peer through the window in the class room door, surveying the dozen or so young faces as they sat pensively behind their desks. "Look at them, "he added cynically. "Butter wouldn't melt. A week from now they'll be answering me back and I'll be chewing their heads off…"

"Oh, it can't be all that bad," I offered and he gave me a sideways glance.

"Which faculty did you say you're from?"

"Faculty?"

"Thought so," he concluded. "Yet, another side-step in the further education system, heaven forbid we should ever get any real lecturers … still, mum's the word, eh?"

At this point, I must confess I hadn't the faintest idea what he was talking about. I was just pleased to have found an ally and together we entered that chamber of horror.

"Good morning," he greeted them. How confident, I thought.

"Morning," I emulated, scanning the room for a suitable chair.

"My name is John Philips," he announced to the class, I shall be taking you this period, and this is…?"

"Er, Cameron Stone," I told him, slipping hurriedly towards a vacant desk. Opening my bag, I removed a notepad and equipped myself with a pen and ruler. Phillips watched me with intrigue, glasses slipping from the bridge of his nose as he regarded me as an owl to a slinking cat.

"You're a student?"

"Yes," I admitted sheepishly.

"I thought …" he began.

"I know," I tried to explain, "I thought, too..."

Philips allowed himself a smile.

That first period involved an introduction to global biomes and the varying methodology of species distribution. It was all interesting stuff, I thought, taking a moment to glance at my new classmates. Hardly any of them looked a day over fifteen, although in truth they were nearer eighteen, the next eldest being a seasoned 22-year old. They were a mixed bunch and I knew it would take time to get to know them.

"Look at the bumpers on that one then!"

It was often a challenging statement, not least when he was preoccupied in the college car park. A large and loud extrovert character who liked fast cars and fast women, so he would have us believe. Jez had a penchant for both engine capacity and breast size, both items being a blurred amalgamation of the two. So we would look, not especially in appreciation of his subject - be it flesh or mechanical, but we would look. "Luscious!" Jez would approve and we found ourselves grinning and cringing with embarrassment.

"Yer'all mouth," Pamela would scathe, and she was right. Yet she still enjoyed flaunting her ample twin strokes with feminine allure, only to rebuke his lewd attentions with vehement indignation.

"Gizzasnog, then," he would venture, extending his tongue to the air like some enchanted lamprey eel.

"Bog off, you perv," she would retort while her soul mate, Susie, tittered effeminately beside her. Mammarially challenged, however, Susie possessed neither the cubic nor the chassis capacity with which to whet Jez's hormonal appetite, despite her interest in this big talker from Torquay.

Such was the ambience of the class, indeed almost the entire academic institution. The transition from child to adult, as always, was preoccupied with identity, with hormones, with masculinity and femininity, with hard drinking binges, discotheques and pot. Indeed, their social development often took priority over their academic ambition. Institutions such as this were the adventure playgrounds of adolescence.

"So, what d'yer do?"

It was bound to come eventually. I had kept quiet for several weeks and had managed to avoid discussing my personal life.

"Civil service," I told them, supping from my polystyrene cup. "I'm retired now though."

"What did you do?" asked Tris. A quiet, shy youth, Tris was a likeable chap. Bright as a button, his only impediment was his low self-esteem. Often he would sit hunched-shouldered at his desk in front of me, his writing pad secreted somewhere beneath his armpit; a writing style that equalled the dexterity of some arachnid paraplegic.

"Oh, all sorts," I offered lamely, "security mostly."

The student lounge was a popular venue during lunch, although I rarely ventured there, preferring the company of my car and radio. It hadn't always been this way. Keen to mix and to get to know my new colleagues, my first visit had been an uncomfortable one.

The air, rich with sweet smoke, bore the assailing scent of cannabis as the odd rolled-up joint was shared sociably among clusters of young people. Easy, Stone! I told myself, almost twitching with forced constraint - *Easy!*

I had entered this world of academia with an open mind. Student venues were synonymous with casual soft drug abuse, so it came as no surprise to witness it, its presence perhaps more tolerable here than prurient. For me, however, the challenge was far more than just academic; I had to resist the years of training and experience that had become second nature to me.

Barely a year ago I would have arrested them. Barely a year ago I would have seized the drug and dragged them off to the nearest police station. Now, however, I no longer bore that burden of responsibility, but I could remember a time when former colleagues were even more zealous than I…

Sunlight filtered through the tall planes that bordered Hyde Park. Cars fought for every yard of tarmac just beyond, while two police vehicles, a van and a car waited beside the curb in the South Carriage Road; their occupants watching pensively at the crowd below.

There were perhaps a hundred black faces lazing in the warm summer sun beside the Serpentine. They were in a relaxed mood, listening to music, playing football, smoking cannabis from homemade reefers that hung from indolent lips.

"Hallo, officer," one man approached us, "we're joost 'av'in' a good time. All is cool in Babylon." Like many Rastafarians, he wore his dreadlocks like a tired mop, his black, yellow and green knitted hat perched almost comically on his head, perhaps infusing a special brand of tea.

"Hello, mate," I attempted a smile. "It's cool," I tried to sympathise, "and I know you're just having a good time, but the problem is the ganja. This is Hyde Park, not Montego Bay." Throwing back his head, his face peeled to reveal a fine set of ivory teeth and his laughter was loud and ebullient.

"Ah know it's Hyde Park," he told me. "If it were Montego you would not be 'ere, an' we'd be on the beach in the sun, you know what a mean? *Hot* sun, not this stuff 'ere… this is not *hot*. We's joost relaxin' an' trying to t'ink we're on the beach – in Montego Bay!" He laughed again, and it was impossible not to laugh with him.

He was a likeable bloke, and maybe over a pint of ale we could have shared a yarn or two, but sadly it was not to be. Our cultures were poles apart, and when it came to flouting the law policemen in London were less known for their sense of humour. But we were grossly outnumbered. Arresting even one of their number for possession of an illegal substance could have caused a small riot, such was their reputation and they knew it. Like a herd of wildebeest visiting a waterhole, safety in numbers was their game as we watched with impotence.

"No Trojan units are available at present," the reply came on the police radio. "Is it urgent?"

"Negative, MP," I told the operator. "We'll remain *in situ* and monitor the situation."

Sometimes a police presence, even a small one such as ours, was enough to remind them they were being watched, sowing a seed of anxiety in their illegal activities. And in this central London park they were playing away from home, many of them hailing from elsewhere in London. But at least, for the moment, they were not hostile.

Then a police panda car passed us by, turned and stopped nearby, the passenger I recognised from a neighbouring station. Bolting out from the car door, 'H' for Hurricane was a young policeman who had earned a reputation for zeal. Possessing a heart of courage in the face of adversity, H had a habit of going where angels feared – common sense obscured by ardent spontaneity. And we almost ran to contain him, but were a fraction too late. "Cannabis!" he cried, as if all but he were oblivious to the outrage.

Striding off into the thick of the crowd like some mechanical wind-up toy, H entered that arena as a Christian condemned. And the tension was almost palpable; a *frisson* infecting them. H grabbed his man who was surprised and more than a little anxious; ash spilling from his open mouth, the reefer snatched by H's finger tips.

"I'm arresting you on suspicion of possessing an illegal substance," he informed him, quite properly, and the entire crowd stood up, edging closer. "You're not obliged to say anything, unless ..." he began to caution, suddenly aware of his predicament, "unless..." the gravity finally – *finally* beginning to dawn on him. Oh, shit! might well have been a fitting expletive as we went after him, jostled by the crowd.

Despite all his impulse and naivety, many who worked with him respected H. He was devoted to his duty without prejudice or favour, as many of us attempted despite the fickle tide of social resentment; resentment of authority, and yet resentment of its yielding too.

"You can't come in 'ere... go an'pick on s'body else, man!" one of their leaders protested, agitated, grabbing hold of H's prisoner. "Pigs are not welcome 'ere, man." The numbers condensed around us. "We're not botherin' you, s'why yoose pickin' on us blacks?" someone else lamented. "Fuckin' racist pigs," another accused.

"Okay, okay, let's all keep cool." One of my colleagues tried to defuse their growing enmity. It was a tense moment. "You know the score, you know it's against the law to possess cannabis..." Sucking their lips with scorn, as is the way with some Afro-Caribbean people, I was 'eyeballed' malevolently by two large men who stood in my way. H was in danger of being isolated from us, his only aegis. "He's nicked so there's no point in getting the arse." Smoke, drawn from their marijuana roll-ups, was exhaled into our faces as goading, ethereal gauntlets of antipathy. H a slavering dog in a condiment store. "Do you want us to call for back-up?"

"Call it! Call your back-up! So fuckin' what?" Their mood was deepening - a flash of apprehension rippling beneath their hostile veneer. Anywhere else and they wouldn't have cared less. Anywhere else and their mood could have turned very nasty, but today, confrontation wasn't their agenda. They had come to Hyde Park to relax – Rasta style.

Here, in large numbers, they had come to enjoy this temporary haven, a haven from a secular world where white society is dominant, and where culture and tradition often clashed head on with their identity and self-esteem. Historically, their race has been the victim of abuse and persecution. Indeed, today we are still dealing with that stigma, both black and white, and with the residue of malign attitudes that prevail.

In that jostling, daunting melee I felt a colleague grip onto my belt. With several years' service, he was easily the most experienced officer among us.

"When I give the word," he mumbled in my ear, "I want you to grab H and hang on."

Behind me, a handful of policemen had quietly linked themselves to form a crude chain. We were going to be H's lifeline and I was to be at the business end of this rescue mission, but we had to act fast, H's prisoner was beginning to resist violently. "Get your fooking white rasclat nigger 'ands off of me!" the prisoner complained vehemently, eyes wild with anger. To be called a 'nigger' by a black man was the ultimate insult he could throw at you, especially if you were black too. He was a stalwart of their group, his street credibility threatened by H's unremitting clasp.

"Now!"

Suddenly, I raised my knee and stamped my boot *hard* against every toe, every shin and every shoe that lay between us, my victims recoiling with pain and alarm as I quickly shouldered them. Prising a fissure between Cerberus and the Minotaur, I lunged at H, grabbing his arm. I had barely caught hold of him before we were heaved, our ragged blue line pulling explosively. H the cork in the proverbial bottle, still attached to his quarry, his quarry attached to the crowd, and for a moment they stumbled and slithered, until their strength finally checked us. Our chain collapsing as H's prisoner finally wrestled free.

The link was broken, but I didn't care, we had H back with us, our momentum dragging him backwards.

"I'll 'ave you instead, then ..." I vaguely heard his immortal words as he grabbed another, and that sudden tack caught us all by surprise, the crowd still recovering their senses. But they were too late. We had stolen the initiative as we bundled both him and his new captive into the van. "You're not obliged to say anything..."

The doors closed and we left - quickly.

An hour later and H's prisoner was released on bail to await the result of the analyst report on the cannabis he possessed; released to rejoin his friends at 'Montego Bay'.

Of Fate and Sentiment

Far below, far from the emollient sun where *erica* frock the feet of granite rock, where gorse thickets bearded by wisps of fleece from errant sheep, pricked their rash of lutein bloom. Far below, far in vale and cleave and combe, ethereal mists lapped the arboreal fabric and consumed the cortex stem, braiding leaf and fern and fungi and their arachnid nets of dew.

The nimble prints of deer had spotted the dank grass margins, their only trace save for a hazel coppice blanched by a grazing doe. And among the fallow pasture, where field mushrooms forced their heads o'er hirsute tussock fists, their fruit canopies would swell as large as dinner plates.

"Are they edible, dad?"

"Dunno," I teased, adding butter to the frying pan. The fruit bodies of *Agaricus* freshly picked and washed were piled on the kitchen surface. "They look like mushrooms, don't they?"

David wasn't so sure.

"They could be poisonous," he warned, quite sensibly. They could, indeed, had I not checked and double checked their identity from my field guide, but nothing remotely poisonous came close to their shape of gill, cap, stem or ovum. Had I been remotely uncertain, then a provident spore check – leaving the cap to drop its coloured spore signature overnight on plain white paper might have resolved any doubt.

"Do you think they're poisonous?" I asked Anna, the fungi sizzling deliciously as I placed them into the pan and her ponytail swung as she shook her head. "Sure?" She shook her head again. "What about you?"

But Edward just stared with wonder.

"You go first, dad," John wisely suggested, "and we'll follow if …" he trailed off.

"If what?" I baited. "If I die a horrible, disgusting death?"

"Give them to the chickens," Edward finally decided.

We sat up at the kitchen table, our plates piled with the chocolate brown flesh of mushrooms oozing with hot butter, and the children hesitated as I ate with gusto, filling my mouth with large chunks.

"You're right to question if they're edible," I told them. "If you're in any doubt then don't eat it," I advised, tucking into more. "The secret is to learn how to identify them properly. Half the fungi in this country aren't poisonous," I went on. "It's just that we're all so used to buying food from a supermarket in neat plastic containers, we've lost our way with nature…" I coughed dramatically. A choking fit that could have stolen any Academy Award and their faces were awash with concern and anxiety as I slumped from my seat, leg twitching to the floor.

"Let's grab dad's while he's not looking," Lucy whispered, betraying my act as she stabbed her fork into my remaining breakfast.

"Oi!" I protested, my recovery miraculous as I climbed to my chair and the kids were quick to see the fun, following her raid on my prize.

As I walked the dogs high along the hill's copper spine I turned my collar against the onset of winter, a chill wind biting at my ears as I paused, climbing a rock to admire the view, the valley transformed into a gold and amber carpet, the boughs of naked trees spreading their branches to the feral sky, the contorted limbs of sessile oaks dominating the gulf, yet here and there the dark and shaded spectres of birch appeared as smoky clusters against the canvas. A cobalt smudge tracing the horizon, forging the battered shore.

What if the air were salted water, I fancied, the land its ocean bed; we the fauna that dwell beneath. The birch the brown wrack weed of this deciduous sea; the valley rifts as *Quercus* coral, the hills as *petraea* reefs that rake the scudding cumuli; clippers of the vaulted pool abound some ephemeral voyage of adventure.

What if?

"Bloody' ell!" Jez gushed. "Look at them tits!" The Friesian cows being the owners of his delight, lowing plaintively as yet another herd of students were rounded to the observation area. Their calves suckled gleefully from opulent udders and Susie began to wish she had inherited a more bovine lineage.

"These calves are just a day or two old," the lecturer informed us, hands buried in the pockets of his overalls, feet clad in large wellington boots. "Within six hours of birth," he continued, "it's essential that the calf feeds on its mother's colostrum."

"Is that Latin for tits," Andy smirked, one of Jez's cohorts.

"No," the lecturer told him pointedly, "more the content. Colostrum is the first milk the mother produces for her offspring and it's full of antibodies that help the calf resist infection and disease. I suspect all of you were fed on your mother's milk when you were born for exactly the same reasons - even you, Andrew."

Pamela put up her hand.

"How much does it suck - drink," she enquired, keen to avoid exciting the boys.

"Six percent of its bodyweight," he told her. "About three litres worth - now, two major health problems can affect a calf. Anyone know what they are?"

We all remained silent, except Tris. He was the only student among us who held a farming background.

"Scouring?" he offered timidly.

"Yes, that's one," the lecturer confirmed. "The other is pneumonia. So what's scouring then, Tris?"

Tris receded behind his long fringe, shifting awkwardly on his feet. He hated being the centre of attention.

"When they lose condition," he mumbled.

"And they usually lose condition if we change their feed too early or if the calf is placed under stress…"

Later, we were to cover methods of keeping sheep and pigs too. These introductions to the basic care of farm animals were important, important if we were to have any clue at all about the challenges affecting farming practices. Few of us had any agricultural experience, a sparse affinity with cattle and yet despite this handicap we, as students, shared a common interest. That interest was the countryside, how it worked, how it sometimes didn't, studying the many influences, political, social, economical, historical and contemporary, that prevailed.

Farmers have created our countryside, making it the way it is - not as some wild and untamed venue of nature. Indeed, that concept was long made redundant by our Celtic, Saxon and Nordic forefathers who needed lumber for fuel and construction, and land to farm, razing a landscape of feral woodland that once harboured beasts like bears and wolves. Indeed, the word 'field' we adopt from the Viking description 'feld', a clearing. Over English history, the land became a labour inherent, the contemporary mural of fields and hedgerows enclosed by a political economy, existing today by providing food for our communities and refuge for our remaining wildlife too. Such 'species rich diversity' depends on good agricultural practice to maintain the countryside we consider so iconic.

In the cow shed, the lesson covered the dairy herds, the roll of the beef and suckler herds (associated with hill farming), the various breeds relating to temperament, characteristic and hardiness (natural resistance to harsh climate conditions), and their sexual maturity. Including the controversial 30 month finishing (slaughter) age imposed by BSE *bovinespongiforum* legislation, the alarm about E-coli and GM *genetically modified* foods. These alone were bitter blows for agriculture. We didn't know it then, but for some, the plague of foot and mouth that subsequently followed was to be their *coups de grâce*. These were tough times.

From our viewing platform we left the relative comfort of that nursery arena to huddle in the cold, outside; our coats drawn tighter about our frames; our warm breath billowing like volcanic geezers while a few erupted with tobacco, wallowing in their sulphurous smog.

Beyond the concrete apron in a corner of the yard, one of my colleagues spotted a carcass, the body of a female calf briefly deposited and awaiting removal. Life and death, it occurred to me, were the standard themes of agriculture, the farmers the inured veterans of their charge's health and suffering that were vulnerable to its fickle plot. The condition of their stock often reflected their success. Indeed, their livelihood depended on it, their beleaguered industries the exiles of romantic vogue and ignorance. To many of us, however, the animal's small body was a forlorn sight, a sight that never failed to pluck the chord of sentiment…

I broke the glass with my police truncheon, the small pane shattering into tiny shards that bounced and chimed a discordant shower, some entering inside, others glancing one hundred feet from wall and drainpipe, ringing the girders of metal steps beneath my feet.

The main entrance door to the flat was so securely locked, there was no alternative but to force an entry from the back via the external fire escape. The window held a narrow frame and once I had removed the jagged edges I stripped down to my shirt and trousers, removing all encumbered articles such as hat, coat, tunic, handcuffs and stick, even my torch - the batteries were close to redundant. And I wormed my lithe physique of nineteen years through that vista of uncertainty.

It was dark inside and as my hands discovered the floor, glass splinters shredding my palm and fingers, I dragged my legs through the hole, rolling on the carpet only to collide ungainly against unseen furniture.

"Hello," I called out again. "I'm a police officer, I'm here to help you," my ears straining for some sound, some spoor of life. But only the blackness yawned, silent and foreboding.

I found my feet, ornaments spilling from random tenure as I groped blindly for the switch, and on finding it, I braced myself for the vulgar corpse. Always, I later learnt, always the initial sight of death was so invidious. Only once I discovered it, defeating the medusa curse with aegis mind, could I then come to terms with its condition. It may have been hanging for a week. It may have been the victim of attack; the walls and carpet a grotesque viscous tapestry. It may be an innocuous body dressed in sheets upon the bed. Either way, I had to find it and deal with it professionally. I at least could owe its loved ones that.

I glanced behind me to assess the scene; an upturned chair - my clumsy entrance, my cut hand smearing the walls with blood as I search for the light. But there was no sign of violence, no furniture disturbed, no smell, no fumes, no sound – save for a subtle hiss emanating from a closed door. And I bound my wounds with my handkerchief to turn the handle, steeling myself for the image that lay behind as I opened the door, my eyes adjusting to the alien light; the television a crackling box of speckled ghosts that cast their eerie glow, the sofa occupied by some form, a morbid supine silhouette. And my heart leapt.

"Hello?" I called in vain, my fingers finding the switch, the invasive light revealing a girl clothed in pyjamas; pill bottles discarded and empty on the carpet. A note to say she was ending her life. She was indeed a pathetic sight.

I brushed back her long brown hair from her face; a pretty girl, perhaps only 21 and I ached with grief at this tragedy of life. What demon could possess such youth that she should want to destroy herself? What trial, what torment, what mandrake worm had inflicted her fragile mind? Yet, as I searched for a pulse, touching her pallid neck, a bead of saliva seeped from tender lips to dribble, then hang by a mucus thread to the cushion below her head.

She was alive!

"Ambulance, please," I reported into my radio, "an overdose, female unconscious."

Gently I placed her head to one side and her snore was rasping, typical of a comatose state. Taking the empty pill pots and her note as evidence, I then embraced and lifted her as some flaccid doll, an angel in my arms as I carried her to the entrance, remembering the door was firmly locked; this was no feeble attempt at suicide.

But fate struck the moment I chose to lower her to the floor, kneeling to place her into a recovery position while I searched the room for the key. And it happened suddenly and without warning - like a gunshot.

The door exploded behind me, the entire brass lock detaching inches above my head to fly across the room. It travelled with such force that it smashed an ornamental plate that hung against the opposite wall, and several faces appeared from the demolished wood as I flinched protectively across my ward. They were firemen, one with a sledgehammer and he grinned madly.

"Oh, 'ello mate," he greeted cheerfully, "they didn't tell us you was in 'ere."

From the hospital I informed her next of kin, returning to her side as she regained consciousness. Watching as she opened her puff eyes and looked about, seeing the nurses, the doctor, the monitor beside her bed. Finally her sight fell on me, a young man in police uniform - naive and stupid though I was to hope for some ounce of appreciation. Instead, she glared at me as some eldritch mamba.

"Fuck off, you bastard!" her venom spat.

The air almost throbbed as it flew across the workshop floor, missing Jez and Andy by a fraction, the lump of wood crashing against a display of tools that hung against the wall.

"Shut it, an' pay attention!" snarled Mr McVitee, a Scot with attitude, his wild hair tamed only by an elastic band that confined it to a pony tail. He was our practical lecturer, taking pains to introduce the basics of health and safety regulations. That is, until his two victims decided to strike up a conversation.

"Rule number one," he informed us as we stood within the workshop, clad in overalls, steel toe-capped boots, goggles, gloves and hard hats. "Always wear adequate safety clothing." He waved his pencil like a baton, striding up and down as he gathered his thoughts. "Rule number two. Always read the hazard warning signs - and abide by them!"

Susie flinched as he raised his voice. "Rule number three - *you two!*" He stabbed his pencil point towards Jez and Andy and they looked like they would burst into tears. "Yes, you!" Mr McVitee went up to them, thrusting his awry beard into their spotty faces and they could almost taste the coffee he had for breakfast, a trace of brown sauce still attached to his whiskers. "What's rule number three?"

Andy opened his mouth, closed it, and then shook his head.

"Dunno, sir," Jez admitted reluctantly.

"Rule number three, *gentlemen*," the word sticking to his sulphur teeth, lowering his voice to emit a growl. "Don't mess with Mr McVitee."

Wearing a stern expression he turned, arms behind his back, giving me a sly wink of alliance as he resumed his lecture. Away from the classroom and workshop, however, away from the strain of keeping order among the tomfoolery, the tiresome quips and the wandering juvenile minds, Mr McVitee was actually a nice bloke.

"Ah have to put them in their place now and then, yer understand," he once told me privately, the words disgorged as quarried phlegm. "Ah'm all heart really," he explained. "Ah care for them, ah just can't abide some o' these young muppets we get from the schools these days – full o' gob wi' very little brain." I smiled, enjoying his laconic description I considered so very apt.

"You were a policeman, is tha' right?" I nodded. "I have a nephew in the Manchester force, just now. He loves it, so he tells me. So where were you?"

"London."

"Is tha' right?" His brow raised and meshed, a spark of sympathy glazing his eyes. "Did you enjoy it?"

"Sometimes," I shrugged.

"Aha, an' sometimes not," he finished my sentence, and then shook his head gravely. "Ah couldn't do that job," he told me. "Don't take me wrong, yer understand, someone's got to do it. Ah just know I couldn't. But if no one did it, then we'd all be in the shite," he went on. "So tell me, what does a London rozzer like you think of life here in Devon – and as a student! It's a bit different for you, eh?"

"You could say that," I told him with diplomacy. "But I love the countryside and I enjoy the study subject."

"You do? That's good, yer certainly doing well enough. So what d'you see yerself doin' when yer done here?"

"Not really sure," I admitted, "maybe a Ranger." But McVitee shook his head.

"Not with a diploma, Cameron," he advised, "God knows why. But if that's the way you want to go, then you'll need to go to university."

The Trouble with Pigs

They were funny looking things, a gang of young pigs that bore all manner of black spots and tan patches. Squealing and snuffling the bars of their sty they regarded us warily, some edging inquisitively closer to us, their pink disc snouts testing the air for our scent, 'piggy' eyes roving beneath long ginger lashes. Mum grunting deeply from inside the brick shed, a contralto *mezzo forte* and the piglets scurried back to her.

"What breed are they?" I asked him.

"Them's liquorice," he told me with a twinkle in his eye, amused to perplex us by both his dialect and homespun humour.

"All sorts," Anna translated, her mind more attuned to the pig farmer's subliminal frequency, and he chuckled with glee that she should understand him.

"Young maid's got zum Demshur (Devonshire) in 'er, ah reck'n." But Anna shook her head.

"We're from London," she told him, and he chuckled again.

"Mars more like." His weathered face was as purple as the heather.

"Zee that'n there?" He prodded a sausage like finger towards a piglet. "Tha's a peg, an' zee tha'n there?" I nodded, my brow knitting with confusion. "Well, tha's anuvver peg." He sniggered again, enjoying his own banter at my expense.

"Looks like a bit of Tamworth and Old Spot to me," I revealed, "maybe a bit of Saddleback too," and he looked at me sideways for a moment, his humour evaporating.

"Tha knows a bit about pegs then?"

"Oh, yes," I told him *lex talionis*, "hang my coat on them all the time." And his eyes narrowed beneath the peak of his cloth cap. "Mind you," I couldn't resist it, "I'll have a quick butcher's hook before I put them in the jam jar, otherwise the trouble an' strife won't be best pleased," I gibed, a poor attempt at cockney rhyming slang. "Will a couple of Lady Gadivers do you?"

"That's ten quid," my daughter translated, his face a picture of astonishment.

I stuffed the notes into his fat hand, placed a piglet under each arm and walked off to the car; the little weaner pigs squealing disconsolately.

"Ruddy vurriners," he growled and I grinned as we drove away.

"What shall we call them?" Anna asked, minding our new porkers in the boot of the estate. I hadn't really thought to give them names. "I'm going to call one Scrumpy," she declared.

"Call the other Piggy," I offered, high on originality, but the names stuck.

A few months at agricultural college and my new found academic knowledge had given me the courage to try my hand at pig-keeping. But I hadn't yet learnt how to erect a stock fence; my first attempt being little short of useless. Before the week was out our pigs had escaped, dining happily on the sprouts in our vegetable patch.

"Pigs are out!" A call to arms was declared one morning, just as the kids were ready for school. And as a team we would equip ourselves with boards and dustbin lids with which to push and coax our itinerant swine.

Hector and Hetty, our two white geese, we had already let out and they descended on the scene like a couple of bellicose nags. Hector worrying at our legs while Hetty hissed malevolently by our heels.

"Go away, you stupid birds!" John complained, pushing Hector off with his foot as we surrounded the pigs.

Hiss, went Hetty. *Squeal,* went the pigs, the dogs barking excitedly from the house as Hector tugged at the hem of John's trouser leg. And in the commotion of that vegetable patch John suddenly slipped, falling on to his face in the pig dung, the pigs darting for freedom. Hector went in for the attack, and swiftly I grabbed him by his strong, thick neck, tossing him into the hedge like an old wellington boot.

In that brief diversion, as John picked himself up and rejoined our hue and cry, Hector simply got to his feet, shook his feathers indignantly and waddled to his missus for a honk. 'I'll get him next time, dear,' I imagined him telling her. 'What a brave hubby,' she might say. Piggy and Scrumpy in disgrace as they hid in their shed, door firmly bolted to prevent their escape.

"We'll be late for the school bus," David declared as they brushed themselves down from the ordeal and hurried on up the track, but we tried in vain to clean John's school uniform.

"I stink," he complained, wiping his face with a cloth.

"Don't worry," Lucy reassured him, squirting him with disinfectant as he ran to catch the others, "half your school friends are from local farms. No one will even notice." And as far as we know, no-one did.

"I wonder if they're turning native," I watched after them.

"No…" Lucy studied them, four figures slipping away along the valley. "I don't think so," she said unconvincingly. "Not them…"

"Before you know it," I told her with a grin, "they'll have straws in their mouths and have hair like hay bales saying, 'Orite my luvver?' You wait and see."

That day I found myself visiting an agricultural supplier, a warehouse and yard filled to the brim with animal feeds, equine rugs and sheep drench, chainsaws and brush cutters, pumps, trailers and pig arcs, along with stacks and stacks of fencing materials. It was a farm junkie's paradise and I was the junky, the proud owner of a twelve-volt battery, some wooden stakes, some insulators, a power unit and a hundred metre reel of electric fencing tape. I was going to sort those pigs out, once and for all.

By evening Lucy and I were pink from our labours, and we recovered out on the patio, sipping gin. It was a romantic scene, watching day kiss the night, stars pricking the mysterious vault: bats flitting from tree to tree, the distant lowing of a cow, the bleat of a sheep. Owls hooting, the river babbling, the crisp zap of electricity - the short shriek of a pig, and the aroma of crackling drifting high on the breeze.

To an animal lover, it seemed a drastic thing to do, but the electric fence had done the trick and within weeks both our charges had grown accustom to the wire, avoiding contact, their escapes all redundant events in the past.

Pigs are natural descendants of wild boar, foragers of a woodland habitat. But we did our best to help them live comfortable lives as we fed and watered them, hearing them grunt contentedly as they rooted up the ground, scratched bottoms on large boulders, dozed peacefully in shade beneath the trees and rolled in their glorious mud wallows.

They grew large and lean and we knew the time would soon come to take them to the abattoir. It was a moment I had dreaded, and having begged and borrowed a suitable trailer from a friend, the time came to take them on their final journey of life. If I were a pig, I reconciled I would much rather have a short quality innings than an existence of stale air and impoverished confinement.

Days later I went to collect a bounty of pork all neatly cut and jointed, and our chest freezer groaned with thirty-three stones of best meat. The children sitting at the table, our first homegrown sausages freshly cooked, and they waited and watched once again as chief food tester placed a chunk into his mouth: *Delicious!*

"Poor Pigs 'n' Scrumps," Lucy lamented, "don't you miss them?"

"No way," they announced and they all scoffed the lot.

The river swirled and bubbled, rushing among the rock-littered bed as it wound its way through the wooded vale. Water spewing in torrents, water cascading in small pools as I sat with my dogs beside the bank, watching the kingfisher poised on its perch as he studied the fish that swam below. A flash of riparian blue as it dived into still margins, plunging headlong, a splash of water and wing to emerge triumphant with its *hors d'oeuvre*.

Sunbeams combed the woodland floor, the canopy a rimose emerald spray that leaked a heavenly blue; the river sparkling, the dart and hover of damsel nymphs, the grass snake swimming a serpentine crawl, exploring the banks for frog and vole.

But as I returned to our home, our haven nestled between tree and hill, Lucy showed me an acid letter. And it spoilt the day.

"Dear New Drizzlewick Parishoner" it addressed us. "A number of new people have moved to the parish in recent years and we, the Drizzlewick community, would like to take this opportunity to welcome them. However," (always the '*however*') "we are concerned that people new to the village should fully integrate with the traditions and wishes of the community. We do not like street lights, traffic lights, painted roads or paved footways. This is a rural area where cocks usually crow at dawn and where animals have been known to make a mess…"

No author had dared put a name to the patronising script. It was a cold and insensitive welcome for us and for the growing number of others who had moved in from *outside*: beyond the briar'd hedge, beyond the jagged wall.

I left the busy arterial road, slipping away from London's traffic clamour, the crowded pavements, the thronging shops, to explore my beat along leafy avenues and des res terraced homes; the roar of congestion, dulling to a throb as I wound my way among alleyways and residential streets; watching the odd car that passed me by; watching the postman as he cycled past.

I had already checked the parked cars, noting if any were facing the wrong way down a one-way street. Were any stolen? Were any near a terrorist target? Was the driver disqualified? Resident or visitor? Checking if their tax discs were out of date? And I observed the houses too, some with drawn curtains; shift worker or night owl? Most had doors firmly closed, some had their windows open to the world. But it was as I turned a corner that I noticed something odd; a television and video player stacked behind a hedge waiting collection. There was a burglary in progress and with any luck I would catch them at it.

"Suspects on premises," I whispered in my radio, "12 Saint Paul's Road, silent approach please," my message spurring a police posse to my aid, and I removed the radio battery to avoid making it squawk.

Quietly I climbed the wall and stole my way across the lawn. My heart thumping wildly as I paused, the backdoor had been splintered open by a jemmy. There was movement inside and I braced myself to fight.

There is no knowing who or what was inside. There may be one villain, there may be more, and possibly armed with a knife. But such burdens of anxiety were often lightly weighed. I held the initiative for the moment and could take them by surprise. Through the kitchen window I saw the contents of cupboards and drawers spilled to the floor in their search for valuables, and I saw the figure of a young man enter, tipping the bin, scattering the debris indiscriminately; the plastic liner he wanted as a bag to conceal his spoils.

I struck quickly, sprinting into the house, the thief like a startled animal as I pinned him to the wall.

"Gazz! Gazz!" he screamed for help, trying to worm his way from my grip as I dragged him to the hall. His partner in crime at the top of the stairs, his arms laden with loot, a hi-fi unit, and it came crashing down at me, knocking my police helmet to the floor as I fended it away; my captor punching and kicking me; my arms wrestling violently to control him, grabbing him in a headlock, my free arm wrapping around his mate as he ran down the stairs, and I drove him *hard* against the wall - he squealing - me growling, and the adrenaline flowed thick and strong.

But it was difficult to control one, let alone two and Gazz escaped, bolting off through the door while I placed my prisoner in an arm lock; handcuffing his wrists through banister rails. "You're nicked!" I snarled in his face, in no mood to faff about.

"Fuckin' pig!" he spat, his words fermenting as I left.

His crony had made a good hundred yards, a darting figure ahead of me as I gave chase, running after him along the road.

"Chasing suspects!" I yelled into my radio. "Male, white, six foot, twenty years, black jacket, Saint Paul's, heading north!" But in the heat of the moment I had forgotten to replace the battery that lay in my pocket, my commentary unheard. The cursed microphone some tormented bungee that danced from my lapel.

"Right, right, right into Barnet Lane!" I continued, running past cars that had slowed to stare and drive away. Running past houses, past gardens, past the postman that walked his rounds, past the dog that barked his warning cry. "Left, left, left into Stanley Drive!"

My colleagues had arrived at the burgled house, removing my prisoner to their waiting car. "Cameron, where are you?" But I couldn't hear them, my radio was dead, my mind focused on the race to catch my thief.

"London Road!" I panted, gasping for air. "London Road!" The pavements crowded, the shoppers browsing their window fare. Running along the tarmac, threading among the traffic until my suspect finally slowed. I was gaining, lungs heaving as I burst into a sprint.

I demolished him like a rugby prop forward, sending him sprawling to the ground and he fought like a wild cat, desperate to escape; heads colliding - trading blows - pinning him to the pavement as he writhed beneath. And as we wrestled, as our arms locked in combat, people stepped over us and just walked on by...

"Bells are up an' sally's away!"

Released from its tenuous perch, the three-ton bell swung from its fixings in the belfry. Its hammer thumping against iron walls to declare a deafening peel, and each neighbouring bell followed in sequence, each released to swing in rehearsed choreography, the ropes controlled by a subtle lengthening of pull, an adept tweak of the sally; the clashing of titanic heads tamed to music. It took effort and concentration; over a year of practice before my ears gradually became attuned to their harmonic arrangement.

"Are you all settled in down at Tanglewood?" Hyacinth enquired when the bells were set once again to enjoy a moment of respite.

"Yes, we love it," I told her.

"Does the children like their new schools?"

"Very much," I revealed. "The schools here are busy but they seem less troubled somehow and the kids less pressured by material values than those we knew in London."

They all nodded for a moment, digesting this piece of news in a way that priests absorb confessions. But I wanted to know as much about them. "So how's things with you, George?"

"Oh, much the same," he coughed. "Still 'ere."

"Farm going well?"

"Could be bett'r," but that was all he would commit. Arthur said nothing, finding a thumbnail to pick. Socialising was hard work. They were all pretty reticent at the best of times but getting any conversation out of them lately was proving a mammoth task. Then I studied their faces, their eyes ringed and hollow and I understood.

"And you, Hyacinth?" I enquired gently. "Finished lambing?"

"Just about," she told me with a sigh, smiling wanly. "Another few days, ah reckon, avore I drop," and they all nodded with empathy.

For much of the year little happened among the sheep farming cycle other than the routine of winter feeding. There was drenching - preventing worms and lice, dagging - removing soiled wool at the rear end to prevent blow fly maggots eating in to them, shearing and maintaining their cloven hooves that were susceptible to foot rot. There was the odd market day too, but sheep breeding was probably their biggest headache.

By spring, summer and sometimes autumn, lambs were being born in barns, in 'in-by' land close to the farmstead where the quality of grass helped to improve the ewe's condition. And if a ram got loose, a lamb could be born just about anywhere, even in winter in a ditch upon the moor, although few would survive the harsh climate.

Lambing time in spring was often an exhausting period, supervising ewes and their new born lambs at all hours of the day and night, there was little room for sleep. Indeed, I was amazed they had appeared for bell practice night. So loyal were they to their bell ringing, to their community and their way of life.

"How'z your studies going, Cam?" George asked. They were keen to learn about us, not necessarily interfering but perhaps a more healthy regard.

"Very well," I reported, "I'm thinking of transferring to a higher diploma at university." And George's eyebrows arched with interest.

"Good for you," he encouraged, "any idea o' a career?"

"Might try the Ranger Service here on Dartmoor," I tested, but their response took me a little by surprise.

"It's a good job if you can get it," Arthur told me, hesitant, glancing wearily at his contemporaries as he struggled to paint a diplomatic slant. "Seems ever'one wants to be a Ranger these days, but not many gets the chance."

Silent and now edgy, Hyacinth studied me as if she were examining a curio in bric-a-brac shop.

"Know much about the National Park?" she asked me.

"Do a bit at college."

"Uh," she bridled, "I've known 'em since they started back in the vivties. Right waste o' time," she said plaintively. "They should nivver 'ave called it a Park," almost wagging her finger at me. She was always a kindly sort, but this subject had rankled her. "People cum 'ere from..." she hesitated, about to say 'London' but thought it impolite, "from all o'er an' treat it like an urban park."

"Thems from Plymouth an' Exeter's wusser," George added pragmatically, but Hyacinth didn't listen, she was on her soap box.

"They drops their litter. An' cattle 'n' ponies get it stuck in their gut. They lets their dogs run in my fields scarin' my yaws (ewes)." She waved her arm vaguely at the tower wall. "They even took the stones from my neighbour's wall – God knows why - for their blummin' daft rockeries I suppose."

"Plannin's all a bugger an'all," Arthur pitched in.

"So I don't thinks much o' the National Park, young man," she concluded, "an' there's plenty more 'ere thinks the same."

Her rebuke was in stark contrast to what I'd always believed, scraping ignorance from my skull. If the National Park's ethos was to succeed at all, I later realised, it had to win the confidence of Dartmoor's recalcitrant farming communities - an unenviable, if not impossible task.

A Higher Learning

"**K**eep in low dif. while you're in the yard!" McVitee reminded us above the revving of tractor engines, diesel fumes belching from our elevated exhausts, and we all engaged the low differential.

The old Ford I drove had an obstinate clutch, which I cursed at regular intervals until its cogs finally meshed, the tractor lurching into action, my whitened knuckles on the wheel. It wasn't a huge gulf from driving a car, only higher up, wider and with more knobs and gear levers than you could shake a stick at.

Twice around the yard, first forwards, then backwards and we were allowed to hitch up to our trailers. Mine the biggest and ugliest, endowed with a staved-in backend and a tyre that bulged with a dromedary hump.

Once attached we all set about reversing, positioning our trailers into narrow bays that were walled with cones and old rubber wheels, and we chugged happily from one to the other, brows knitted with concentration. My foot dancing on the pedals as I double declutched, revving hard to adjust the transmission, missing it, pulling back the lever to crunch it into place.

My trailer possessed an obstinate pivot, the wheel hobbling, its inflamed bunion slapping the ground with each wobbled turn. But despite the handicaps, despite the awkward angles and some anxious events, we all managed to survive that trial by tractor. Indeed, some of us might even admit to enjoying it.

Later that day we all wore the white coats of laboratory assistants, all breezing in like starched ghosts as we gazed the table fare. An assortment of grasses lay on one side of the room, a selection of winter twigs on the other while various fungi, lichens and liverworts occupied a surface in the centre.

"You've all got thirty minutes to identify these species," Philips announced, examining his watch. "You should all have a reasonable grasp of the subject by now, but you may use the field guides provided if you need them."

I hovered around the winter twigs and at a glance I knew most of the selection. Many of the fungi types I recognised too, but it was the grasses that gave me the hardest test, their ligule shapes, blades, stems, stalks and seed heads all subtle variations of each other. A few obvious ones, such as cocksfoot, timothy and common couch I could distinguish, even then I sometimes got it wrong. My colleagues just as challenged as I, so when our lecturer abandoned the class for a few minutes, a few of them resorted to adolescent forms of entertainment.

Someone lobbed a piece of fungi and Jez retaliated, a sticky bud propelled through the air. Missing its desired target it bounced from the wall, then a glass receptacle, before attaching itself to Pamela's hair.

"Oh, piss off!" she retorted, removing the offending article to return the serve. The whole class was reduced to juvenile dereliction within seconds, pieces of plant material flying in all directions; yours truly a stoic island of sanity and patience amid the fray, calmly identifying their projectiles as they landed nearby.

Being the only very mature student in the class I often found myself alone, neither totally accepted by my younger fellow colleagues nor completely affiliated with the staff. To some I was a sort of father figure, someone whom they could approach for advice, but at other times my isolation would prove too much that and I found myself slipping into the odd moment of madness.

"Philips!" I teased and the youngsters scurried to their tables wearing nonchalant faces. They were just like my children. "Only kidding," I grinned, only to become the target of the remains.

Philips soon returned to the room and they returned to their tables once again while his eyes roamed the students, the tables and the laboratory floor; his gaze fixing on my balding pate adorned with cornucopia.

"Everything okay?" he enquired cautiously.

"Oh, I think so," I told him. "Don't you?"

As I reflect on that year at agricultural college, my feelings are mixed. I had learnt a great deal about the care of livestock, about soils, flora and fauna. About government policy, organisations and agendas, about trends and market influences. The diversity of wildlife habitats, the farming practices good and bad. And Mr McVitee's practicals too were invaluable - the use and maintenance of rural tools and machinery, basic woodland management and the eventual building of stock fencing. To me it was all interesting stuff, but I quickly tired of the juvenile raucousness, the anguish of the teachers and the general chaos of college life.

Mindful of McVitee's advice, I decided to transfer to a university that boasted a higher example of rural management, and my academic challenge started all over again.

Perhaps here within this university faculty, with its hallowed courtyard embroidered by Boston ivy, with its lecture theatres and classrooms, some of them bleak and sombre venues, the students a little older, a little more studious, perhaps here I would rise to greater things.

"Bollocks!" Becky declared petulantly, stamping her black leather boot against the floor, her face bristling with pierced rings and studded stones, 'Ban Blood Sports' emblazoned on her denim coat. "Where the friggin' 'ell is room N 23?"

"North block," I told her, examining the map, "on the left." And she stormed off, all boots and pink leggings, her lime green frock a cheese-cloth rag about her waist. I followed in her wake, across the courtyard, up the stairs and along the corridor before she stopped and turned to face me.

"You followin' me, or what?" she challenged, her features a jangling symphony.

"Rural Resource Management?" I gently enquired.

"Yeah," she confirmed, thrusting her chin like an anvil, nose and bottom lip stapled by filigree.

"Me too," I told her with a smile and her frown deepened, her needle eyes threading the sober space between my head and shoes.

"Bollocks," Becky declared again, almost with regret, then turned and pushed open the door.

It takes about six months to settle in to a new establishment, I discovered, six months to learn the geography, to understand their system and their peculiar ways; six months to grasp what they want from you and whether you can cope, and time to establish relationships with new colleagues and lecturers. But I found myself hovering once again, glancing through the door window to watch the curried assortment of students seated in that class and I felt my stomach knot. It was a daunting prospect fraught with uncertainties.

"You a new Rummy?" A voice came from behind, a bearded lecturer his arms burdened with a stack of pamphlets.

"No, I'm a student," I announced, keen to avoid repeating the mistakes of the past.

"Really?" the lecturer replied with sarcasm. "I would never have guessed." And I entered once more into that chamber of horror.

As I first entered that room, I quietly rejoiced to find several other mature students, although I was still the elder, a few following close on my heels.

I nodded at a bespectacled hippy; long hair, John Lennon glasses, goatee beard and knitted waistcoat. He nodded at me, mister conventional; short hair and sweater.

"Hi, I'm Boris," said a neighbour as I found a seat, Boris a skinhead with ringlets through his nose, and I imagined he and Becky shackled romantically by their entangled hoops.

"Todd," introduced another, a handshake like a wet fish, but his fingers bore the rough skin of labour, his forearms a muscular testament to hard graft.

There were others too, a gaggle of teenagers who dominated one side of the room; boys fresh faced with bum fluff and two girls in crop tops, the odd pustule to compliment their hormonal rush. As 'oldies' of 26-years plus, our group appeared as a collection of lost misfits, wandering abroad life's tortuous route.

"Good morning," the lecturer welcomed, adjusting his work on the overhead projector. "My name's Brian Hicks, I'm in charge of your first module and we'll be discussing landscapes, what they are and why we feel they are important - or maybe not so important to the rural environment," he began.

This subject was more high-brow than my former experiences, the lecturer more relaxed, more polished, more in control. "Oh, by the way," he added with a wry smile, avoiding my eyes. "A Rummy is an RRM student - *Rural Resource Management*, as opposed to a Remmy - *Rural Estate Management*, or an Agi - *Agriculture*. It helps to amuse us, so bereft are we of such wit and entertainment at this faculty," he went on, "so Rummies is what you is. Nothing whatsoever to do with the Royal Navy, bless their cotton socks, nor is it a popular card game sometimes endured in the smoke-filled corners of the student bar..." He was quite a character.

Afterwards, in the student lounge we enjoyed our coffee break huddled around low tables as the game of introductions, pecking order and social acceptance become the priority.

Boris and the hippy seemed to be hitting it off well, both sharing the same mix of tobacco and marijuana, its sweet aroma making my police nostrils twitch. My student brain, however, had grown so accustomed to such activities I no longer considered them quite so offensive.

"This'll do me," Boris announced, smoke curling from his mouth. "Glad to get away from London. So much shit there, things were getting pretty hot."

We all nodded as if we knew what he was talking about, although I doubted any of us had the faintest idea, perhaps other than the hippy. Happy to sit and do little else, he expelled smoke like a dragon on heat.

"I'm Cameron" I introduced myself.

"Cool," the hippy returned, saying nothing else. He was an odd character. Indeed, just the look of him was odd.

"Do you think you'll like it here?" I pressed, but it was hard work.

"Maybe," was all he mumbled. Probably stoned out of his mind, I thought.

"What did you do?" asked Todd, biting a lump from his cheese roll.

"Six months," said Boris. "Should have been twelve but the Screws let me out on good behaviour."

We all fell silent for a while as I scooped up my heart from the floor.

"No," Todd corrected, his mouth full of bread, "I meant for a living."

"GBH," said Boris, without a blink of an eye. "You?"

"JCB," Todd told him. "Do the odd contract," he went on between masticated bouts. "Dig up the dirt, then fill 'em in," he placed his fist against his breakfast to emphasise the point. In that moment Todd had revealed sharp wit and alacrity and I warmed to his character. Slow to realise it, it took time for Boris to appreciate the ridicule, and he fell silent as his skull radiated heat from a fermenting mind.

"Bollocks," said Becky, fiddling irritably with one of her adornments. "Fuckin' thing's giving me right aggro." But few of us showed any sympathy. Becky tugging painfully at her nose, finger inserted to test the stud fixing, and her eyes crossed together as she attempted to focus. And I couldn't resist a grin of amusement.

"You laughin' at me?"

"Sorry," I told her, "but you do look funny."

Surprisingly, Becky didn't take offence. She seemed to respect honesty in its innocuous form and I almost detected a smile.

"I knew this geezer in the Scrubs," Boris piped up again, "got done over, so 'e stuffed this knitting needle through the wanker's nose." We all winced, as we must.

"Knitting needle?" enquired Todd. "That's a bit wussy, isn't it? Why not a knife or a skewer?"

Boris looked at him beneath a glaze of enmity.

"'Cause he wasn't in the kitchens when he done it," Boris growled.

"These knitting circles can get real nasty," I quipped.

Boris left us in a huff. "Wankers," he said, leaving the hippy to suck alone at his skinny reefer.

"Oh, bollocks!" cried Becky, her voice unusually anxious, blood streaming from her nose, dripping from her studs, her rings and her chin. Out of habit I kept a clean handkerchief in my pocket, and out of habit I gave her first aid, placing it to her face to stem the flow.

It was dark and I was running, running through jaundiced streets tinged by neon light; running past buildings, past empty cars, past doorways and deserted shops, running to the accident that had raped the night.

A car was on its side, a crumpled, shattered husk. A newspaper van wrapped around a pillar box, its driver dazed upon the pavement, watching, watching as they pushed the car back to its feet and it bounced and trembled until it came to rest. Their friend was inside, his head crushed between shards of metal. But they couldn't get him out. The girl hysterical, clawing at the broken glass to get to him, and I yanked her back.

His skull was fractured, half his head hanging by a thread of flesh, his brain a molasses mulch, blood spewing, and his features bore the strain of imminent death; he a convulsing image of distress as my hands tightened on the door. But it held fast, buckled and warped by impact, trapping him by the neck.

I felt impotent. I could do nothing, nothing save to extract my handkerchief from my pocket to stuff into that hole inside his head. It was a useless gesture and I felt utterly defeated as he twitched and quivered, his face a spasm as life left him, escaping to ethers more divine.

Only as day broke, once we had carried his corpse to the mortuary and all the evidence compiled, the injured in hospital, the accident neatly removed, did I allow myself to suffer. I was stunned to silence as I wrote up my report in the police station canteen.

Face pale, my shirt and tunic still stained with blood as I described the fatac (fatal accident); the witnesses, their statements, the vehicles, the road plan, the action taken; concluding with station officer informed - names and addresses exchanged.

Then briefly I lay my nodding head to the table, exhausted by the strains of the night, then woken by my colleagues who returned jaded and beat. We were the soldiers of society, weary from the strains of policing London, our ordeals as wounds that smelt our minds.

The leaves rustled, the wind whispering, the boughs creaking as the sky darkened. The storm was descending, a gigantic nimbus; a mass of black rain that consumed the horizon. Dartmoor a landscape daunted; the tors as raven heads, unblinking against the slick. Even my dogs walked closer beside me, aware of the tension that had fused the conflicting air.

Then the thunder growled deep and malevolent from the distance as it headed our way. There was nowhere to shelter. The woods and fields were dangerous places in a storm, so I increased my pace, trying to return to our home, lightening bolts creasing the petulant sky. One thousand, two thousand... I counted as I broke into a trot. Three thousand, four thousand... and the thunder roared its mighty wrath. Four miles, I judged. Another few minutes and the storm would be upon us, and the dogs cantered alongside as I thrashed my way though the bracken, tripping on unseen boulders, my boots snagging on briar whips. There wasn't time - I knew... there wasn't time! And the wind blew cold and strong.

The trees creaked and groaned in protest, rocking as if they were at sea, tossed by the force eight gale. And the sky erupted above us, hailstones descending, bouncing from every stone, from every limb. A claw of lightening swiping the turbulent air - Thor's hammer splitting ethereal heads, the chase of the Valkyrie a wretched howl.

My head felt the friction and my hair stood erect; hailstones cascading, the dogs hugging my legs. And I caught a glimpse of some rocks. They were large and tumbled, a great slab leaning against another and I scrambled to it, seeking refuge in the hollow beneath, my canine rugs prostrate about my knees.

As we dripped, as we panted, trees fell around us, their root plates prising the woodland cloth. Branches torn, leaf and limb raining down, and as I watched from our sanctuary - watching in awe, I felt humbled and elated.

It was great to be alive once more!

An Audience of Trials

"Animal welfare has been an emotive issue in this country for centuries," Becky announced, her pierced adornments like heavenly bodies, her chin thrusting at the audience as she delivered her speech. "The British have been well up for it," she went on, "banning cock fighting, dancing bears an' dog fights…"

She was a bright girl, a little headstrong at times but keen to wear her heart on her sleeve.

"Protesters like Greenpeace publicly shamed the fashion industries that marketed animal skins such as mink, stoat and seal. On the TV, images of seals beaten to death horrified the civilised world, provoking a demand for synthetics instead of real fur. But the irony is that by saving the animals, we replaced fur an' fleece with nylon clothes made from oil, the factories pollutin' the atmosphere instead…"

You knew what Becky was about simply by looking at her. You could take her or leave her. That was the way she liked it. Yet beneath the rebel exterior, the body piercing and the up front 'don't mess with me' attitude, Becky, like most of us, was really just a softy.

I once caught her sulking in the corridor, shortly after a fraught telephone conversation with her boyfriend. It was her last.

"Bastard," she complained, "'e never did like the Waltons." A tear escaped and trickled down her cheek. "Just about the only decent thing the American's ever gave us." I offered her my handkerchief, once again, and she took it, wiped her eyes then blew her nose, which wasn't quite what I expected. Screwing up her deposit she handed it back to me. "Ta," she said, and went.

On the overhead projector she replaced the picture of a dismembered seal, blood red against the snow, swapping it for a picture of belching industrialised chimneys. It was Todd's cue and she sat down.

Todd delivered the second piece in our trio effort. "We know that trees are mostly made of the carbon they extract from the atmosphere, pumping out the oxygen and moisture we all depend on."

Todd paused for a moment, losing his place from his notes, and he fumbled in his pockets for the illusive page. Having found it, he carefully unfolded the paper and glanced nervously at the audience before continuing.

"If we burn organic material such as wood, the carbon is released back into the atmosphere without any damaging effect. But fossil fuels such as coal, gas and oil have been trapped beneath the ground for millions of years, the atmosphere above replacing the deficit, maintaining the balance..."

Todd was generally a quiet bloke, a thinker whose intelligence far outweighed the menial labours of his former employment, although his skill with a digger was highly regarded. Naturalising in Totnes since he was a child, his parents were incomers who had long since settled from the wild fells of Cumbria. And I detected the odd northern vowel still prominent in his speech.

"According to the geological clock, the human race has barely existed more than five minutes. Methane, however, has existed beneath the sea for millions of years in the form of organic material transported by rivers and made dormant by cold sea pressure. Carbon sinks such as those of the cold waters of Antarctica or the Amazon rainforest contribute to the natural store released after a geological period of time dramatically influencing climate changes. The sea temperature warms and the stored methane hydrates bubble up to the surface, accelerating the global warming process.

"Scientists have discovered a pattern of such carbon climax incidents over several million years," he went on, "all indicating major catastrophic events such as rising seas and floods." Then ending on a piece of theatre he lowered his voice, the class gripped by the drama. "They believe we are on course for the next climax this century. Indeed, the signs suggest it has already begun. Our carbon emissions may well have triggered global warming prematurely, and it may be too late to apply the brakes. But I think it's about time we all tried – don't you?"

It was a sombre message and as he returned to his seat, I took his place. It was my turn to deliver the conclusion.

"Greenpeace was perhaps the most successful driving force behind the conservation movement that helped shape public minds and attitudes during the Fifties and Sixties," I announced to the class. Glancing at my notes, I slipped a picture of the ship, Rainbow Warrior, onto the overhead projector and noticed my fingers were trembling.

I had cleared out bars full of late night drinking revellers, I had barked across streets at marauding football supporters, and I had cleared away the public from countless bomb scenes. But I had never stood up in front of an audience to give a lecture. Such was the training at university and I was nervous, our tutor assessing us from the back of the room.

"Their non-violent confrontation with authority quickly earned them respect - this and their high media exposure as controversial figures made a huge impact on public opinion. Anxieties about pollution, the mass exploitation of the world's natural resources and the abuse of animals both in the wild and in captivity have influenced legislation to reflect public concerns for the environment in which we live…"

I was conscious of my voice, a dark brown voice that still, out of habit, bore an edge of authority. It was hard to soften it. It was hard to forget.

"I swear to tell the truth, the whole truth…" I announced from the witness box, my deep dulcet tones booming from the audio system as the jury sat attentively across the room. The gallery filled with spectators, the defendant a picture of humiliation, the wigs and gowns of barristers cluttering the tables beneath. The judge, a saturnine image of repose, bereft of sympathy, bereft of character.

Officially known as the Central Criminal Court, The Old Bailey was a very austere building, a venue that would often reduce even the most ardent criminal to timidity. No-one it seemed could escape the atmosphere of severity. Witnesses would sometimes quake under the strain of its *gravitas* and police officers were no exception.

"…as a result of what I was told," I referred to my statement in a typical laconic police style, "I went to the scene and saw this man," indicating towards the defendant, "running from the victim's address, holding a baseball bat - exhibit CS one, in his right hand." I had to pause and speak deliberately to allow my speech to be recorded by the court stenographer, typing silently with skill and speed. "I gave chase, running after the defendant as my police colleagues went to assist the assault victim…"

My evidence lasted some ten minutes in length my voice unfolding the drama as the narrator of a play. The court was silent while I delivered each sentence, a methodical catalogue of facts, the policeman's soliloquy on centre stage. And when I had finished, I braced myself for the theatre of questions, the aggressive cross-examination, the harrying remarks, the needle comments and the derisory defamation that often followed. And my heart pumped wildly, the beat thumping in my ears.

"Constable Stone," the defending lawyer addressed me. "You say you cornered the defendant in a garden, is that correct?"

"Yes, m'lud," I answered to the judge, as is the formality.

"You say the defendant raised the bat in a threatening manner?"

"Yes, m'lud."

"Did he say anything?"

"No, m'lud."

"Then why did you think that he was threatening you?"

"The expression on his face, his aggressive stance, the way he held the bat as if he were about to strike me."

"So you hit him, is that right?"

"I charged at him with a dustbin lid."

"You knocked him down and tried to break his arm!"

"I placed him in an arm lock, yes."

"So you in fact assaulted him, didn't you?"

"In as much as I had to defend myself to arrest him."

"Oh," the barrister raised his eyes in mock belief. "*You* were defending yourself? And here I am, thinking it was the defendant who was defending himself!"

I said nothing, and the judge looked at the defending brief above his glass lenses.

"My lord, it is plainly obvious what happened that night," the barrister went on. "Fearing for his life, the defendant wrestled the bat from the alleged victim, both receiving injuries in the struggle. Then this *yob* in uniform," referring to me, "chased him into a garden and attacked him. That's right isn't it?"

"No it's not, m'lud."

"You assaulted him! You've just admitted it! Your statement to this court is just a pack of lies! Isn't it? *Isn't it!*"

I felt my face glow scarlet from the provocation. Keep cool, Stone, I told myself.

Only ordinary members of the public could display anger, lawyers to boot, such vociferous outbursts were generally accepted; indeed it sometimes added weight to their conviction – but not from a policeman. Policemen had to be calm under pressure. They had to be the models of society who pursue their onerous duty with unswerving fear or favour. Any anger or irritation I felt now I had to bottle up in the name of probity and allegiance to the law. Indeed, suppressing such emotions could sometimes prove too great a burden, not only in the courts but in the impoverished field of duty too; that embattled province of virtue and malice.

"The assault was necessary to overpower him," I replied, my base voice resounding from the audio speakers. "He was violent. He had attacked the victim. He was armed with a weapon and I had to control him before he hurt someone else. If he were not violent, then there would have been no need to restrain him the way I did."

The jury nodded and I took heart from their response. The barrister speechless for a moment, I had verbally punched him with common sense.

"Quite," he said.

The cross-examination lasted several minutes more before the summons of the next witness. But as I was about to step down from the witness box someone beckoned me.

"Officer?"

My God, it was the judge! His Lordship regarding me above half-moon spectacles, his hand urging - what error had I performed, what misdemeanour?

"Y- yes, m'lud?"

It was most unusual, but I went, leaving the box to approach him as the jury watched with interest, as the legal wigs looked on with curiosity, their contrivance disturbed, their act interrupted as I inclined my ear to his stately head.

"Officer," he enquired with a twinkle in his eye, "do you sing?" And I looked at him.

"Only in the bath, m'lud," I was quick enough to rally, and he smiled.

"What a pity," he said. "Anyway, carry on."

Trendlecombe is a small market town on the moor and it's a funny thing but many of its residents bare a similar resemblance to one another. Several generations hail from the region, the Foggins, the Grimms and the Soussons, all endowed with dark curly hair and awry teeth, their genes perhaps a throwback from the Celtic tribes who once lived and reigned among Dartmoor's feral landscape.

It is very difficult to tell which family is which, however, especially for incomers like us. But in the process of time, as farmers who become familiar with the breeds and traits of various sheep, we gradually began to appreciate the various characteristics as our children introduced an explosion of school friends from Trendlecombe market town.

The top lip of a Grimm, we discovered, had a tendency to wander animatedly as they spoke. A Foggin would cock their head as a spaniel in curiosity. But a Sousson would never look you in the eye, regarding the nape of your neck when held in conversation.

"Are you brothers?" I enquired. They looked so alike, and Josh squealed with unrestrained laughter, Joel breaking into a smile.

"Naw," Josh corrected, cocking his head to one side. "E's a Sousson, an' I'm a Foggin,".

"Cousins maybes," mumbled Joel, eyes fixing somewhere beneath my chin. Josh's mouth gaped in mock surprise, revealing a wad of mulched bread. "Yer gert gake!" Joel teased him. "Your nair zistle (near sister) be my mum."

A tall, thin lad of 14, Joel wore clothes too large, flared trousers that flapped against tatty trainers and a shirt devoid of buttons save one that concealed his modesty at the middle, the tail lapping the backs of his thighs. Both boys regarded the world from beneath great mops of dark curly hair, shovelling sausage and beans into their faces while we all sat around the table at our home.

"Yeah," Josh squealed, trying to get a grip of this revelation. "Your dad's a Grimm, more like."

A year or two younger, a foot or two shorter, Josh stuffed his mouth with bread as he conversed in broad Devonian. Perched on his chair with one leg swinging, one arm sloughed about the crockery, it occurred to me that he wasn't accustom to the formality of having meals at the table, preferring to eat on the hoof or snack in front of the television.

"Josh lives on a farm," David revealed proudly.

"Your dad's a farmer?" I enquired with interest. "Sheep?"

"Shape 'n' bullicks," Josh replied. "But me dad's never home. Uncle's runnin' the farm," he explained a little downcast.

"So your uncle and your mum live on the farm?" I enquired a bit too closely and Lucy gave me a sharp kick beneath the table. Half their conversation seemed jibberish, the other utterly incestuous.

"Shaggin' ah reckon!" Joel declared mischievously and Josh glowered at him.

"Your Eve's doin' our Ben," Josh returned, and I thought I detected a slight wince of the lip, the Grimm in him becoming agitated.

"Yes, well, perhaps you boys would like to explore the river after lunch," Lucy suggested, the best distraction she could think of at the time.

"Our Marion's a Grimm," Joel continued unabashed. "An' our Barry's a Foggin." Josh opened his mouth once more, eyes staring from beneath a wild thatch fringe.

"Naw," he denied. "Your Barry's no Foggin… E's a Grimm an' all."

"Purt nare. (Pretty near)."

"Barry's Kate's a Foggin!"

"His Jack's naw, though!"

"Where's 'e to, then? (Where's he from)?"

"Dunnaw," Josh shrugged, resuming their meal as Lucy and I, and the children looked on, stunned to silence.

Their revelation might have been amusing had it not been so disturbing and yet these boys appeared well-fed, their minds and hearts reasonably nourished. They were sometimes disruptive in school, unyielding to discipline, but they were not spiteful or wicked and they got along well with our kids.

"Do you want to be a farmer when you leave school, Josh?" I asked.

"Naw," he told me. "I wanna be a jet pilot."

"You have to work hard at school if you want to be a pilot," I suggested, but Josh said nothing. I was spoiling his dream.

"What about you, Joel?" But Joel just wiped his plate with his bread and shrugged.

"Dunnaw," he said. "Maybes work on a farm. Maybes a lorry driver."

"What d'you do, then?" Josh asked me and it took me a little by surprise.

"Oh, I'm… er, I'm a student," I told him and Joel smirked.

"You too olden," he said.

"Yes, you're probably right," I admitted with a sigh.

"You's from London?" Josh enquired, and I nodded. For a moment they were in awe of their hosts; that they could meet with beings from such an exotic planet let alone eat their sausage and beans for tea - and at a table too!

In the years that followed we were to see more of Josh and Joel, meet a few of their relations and unwittingly rub shoulders with others as we visited the market at Trendlecombe, swam in the pool during summer and attended the school plays; the audience hogging the seating, thronging the doorways, the windows and corridors. The men leaning casually against the walls, locks flowing freely, shirts unbuttoned to the navel, grinning their ivory dominoes while their women cheered and clacked in Devonian consort, blouses strained by their free-ranging breasts.

The Night of the Icarus

It was dark. Burnt by the neon street lights, the stolid silhouettes of terraced houses turn instantly into a blur as I accelerate, and the car engine whined; some mechanical scream of pain as I work the gears. And my blue revolving roof light trails a sapphire ribbon against pavements, wet and glistening from recent rain.

"All units wait!" The message had boomed from my radio. "An ambulance crew require urgent police assistance ... Brockwell Street ... a male berserk with a carving knife ..."

"Five four three nearby, MP!" I had yelled acknowledgement, the microphone still hissing like some demented snake upon my lapel; now a dangling, cackling beast that hung from my belt, the noise blending with the squeal of my tyres as I round a bend.

The police share respect and empathy with the medical services with whom they frequently called upon. Paramedics and their like are the kind and helpful faces in life's harmful trial, so my anxiety to protect them was high.

I saw traffic lights ahead of me, a pair of crimson eyes and I slowed down for the junction, pumping the brakes rapidly to avoid a skid, and the tenement walls pulsated from the wail of my siren call. Streams of headlights approach the junction – stopping as they see me, and with raised hand I thank them, winding the gears once again, pressing my foot to the floor; the engine a high, staccato shriek.

Brockwell Street? Brockwell Street? Wasn't that near that old, rundown place? That hostel, a decadent venue where the low-life dwell, where I arrested that youth a year or two ago? The one who had stabbed his girlfriend, the blade slicing through her arm making it hang, red and raw like a butcher's joint on display... but that's another story, another poignant memory that runs like claret spilled, weaving some fluid path, some course that dwells within those dark and intricate recesses of my brain. Brockwell Street! It was there, and I doubled declutched, dropping a gear, adjusting speed, feeding the steering wheel while the adrenaline began to leak into my arteries with each compounding second.

To prepare myself and 'psych myself up' to deal with any threat I might face, I would squeeze the steering wheel, trying to compress it, focussing my mind, nerve and sinew for duty, bracing myself for whatever danger I might have to face. How many steering wheels I had abused during my police career I have no idea – but it was probably a lot.

Indeed, once so heavily primed for action, it took a great deal of self-discipline to calm down if the incident didn't require it. Some colleagues were better than others at controlling their resolve, all drawing on different strategies they developed with experience. But one thing was certain – to be mentally unprepared could be damaging, especially if taken by surprise.

The incident might be a false alarm. It might be Death's own sickle swiping at my heels, but however gruesome, however terrible the scene might be, I must deal with it, for my kind are all there is ... there is no-one else.

The ambulance stood ominously alone, its doors gaping wide, its bowels yawning like the carcass of some forlorn animal, slaughtered, gutted, and tossed grotesquely for the raven night. Only its blue roof light echoed any sign of life; pulsating, revolving like some lonely lighthouse, casting an eerie tinge against the walls, the buildings, the windows, the many anxious faces that had pressed against the glass. It is fear that jolts us back to our childhood scares. And it was pure, unadulterated fear that had tainted all who had witnessed the event.

"Five, four, three on scene!" I reported into my radio, that querulous beast, now like some demented cat, spitting with static. My breathing was shallow, controlling the fear that was trying to worm its way beneath my shield; a shield of *sang-froid* calm, a shield of courage I sometimes bear when faced with danger or disaster.

"Stone!" an old, die-hard sergeant once regarded me at Hendon training school; me at 18 years of age cross-examined in a make shift court. "Stone, you remind me of a swan," the sergeant informed me. "All calm and collected on the surface ... but paddling like shit underneath!"

I was paddling now.

"He's over there! He's over there!" she pointed, almost hysterical, blood splattered about her face and hair, eyes wide, mouth gaping, stabbing a trembling finger towards a wall, towards the one who had escaped from a secure mental hospital just hours before. Returning to his parents' house, half naked, to cut his wrists with a long kitchen knife as he wrought havoc in their home, the victim had called an ambulance, and the crew were attacked as they arrived. He, deranged, deciding to leap over this high wall to escape, the one I contemplated now - the one that bore an ominous, bloody handprint.

The wall surrounded a garden full of shrubs and trees as I discovered while in pursuit, leaping from the top. Landing with a solid thump upon the grass, I rolled away, my senses acute, hearing only my own heart beat, like some manic death-watch beetle thumping in my chest. Holding my breath for fear that I should reveal myself within the darkness. My radio silenced, the battery detached lest it should betray me to this knife man's fate.

But I could see or hear nothing at first; no movement, no sound, just some distant canine protest, and the scuffing of feet, subtle but urgent.

It was Icarus, the man possessed.

I scaled a fence, the timber groaning beneath me, emerging onto the tarmac road, blinking in the artificial light. I stopped again to strain my senses but there was nothing; no sight, no sound other than the alien wail of sirens, more police vehicles that had found my empty car.

"All units," I whispered into my radio, the battery now in place. "Male with knife lost in cul-de-sac nearby..."

"Which cul-de-sac?" came the reply, an unwelcome, squawking invasion.

"I don't know," I replied curtly, the name sign at the road entrance too far to venture at that moment. "Just north of Brockwell Street."

I glanced beneath parked cars, a favourite hiding place for thieves, only this was no ordinary crime. The gardens too were empty. Where the hell is..?

He was there. I caught a glimpse of him from the corner of my eye; a wretched figure, perched on the roof of a house, clinging to the chimney stack, his naked torso caked with blood; staring down at me like some demonic owl.

The house had three floors, all windows dark and lifeless, and from the attic, a single porthole watched with Hades' unblinking eye. And I feared for those occupants. What had this mad man done to them? And I suppressed the panic, that evil cocktail of adrenaline and bile that was welling up inside me; infecting me as I imagined the carnage. I imagined what macabre secret lay behind its door, and I attacked it, laying into that locked impediment with that thing they call the Commissioner's key - a size 10 boot, kicking hard until the wood gave way. Then I groped in the darkness, unseeing but my nose alert for the stench of death - that taint, that rancid odour of decay. My trembling fingers finding the contours of a light switch.

Then the dull, aching dread as no light came.

He above me. He with the knife. And I grabbed a spade from outside, the metal blade a weapon, my fingers tightening like a vice around its shaft, and I chopped frantically, carving some imaginary path through that molasses, that black and frightening void, lest I should meet him, lest I should confront this crazed and wild-eyed monster – for it is I who must deliver the telling blow! ...

"You alright, Cameron?" Arthur enquired. "You look like you've zeen a ghost."

"Fine..." I told him, temporarily shaking the residue of a memory that haunted my mind. "Fine." And I watched him as he took up position, placing the ball to his chin, eyes fixed on the wooden skittles that occupied the corner of the room. He rolled it with speed and precision, demolishing all but one and our team roared with applause.

"Lucky," the opposition taunted, the opposition being the Young Farmers. Our motley skittles team the Drizzlewick Misfits, and George scraped the score with chalk onto the wall slate.

"Cummon, Nobby," a young woman encouraged, and Nobby alighted from the bench to take his turn. A tall, wiry man in his early twenties, Nobby displayed great dexterity as he held his beer glass in one hand and bowled with the other; the audience enthralled by both his skill at skittles and by the lack of spillage from his jar. He scored a full strike. Minutes later, Nobby repeated the performance again.

The skittles alley belonged to the Cabbages & Kings, Drizzlewick's public house, both regulars and contestants squeezed into the room to witness the great skittles contest. The Young Farmers were winning, leaving the Misfits to ponder over their beer at half time.

"How does he do that?" George enquired at the bar, studying his glass of amber pickle in one hand, an imaginary skittles ball in the other.

"Buggered if I know," said Captain Claret.

"He's well balanced," Nobby's young lady friend explained, overhearing their conversation. "You know?" And she smiled lewdly, placing her hands about her loins as if she were clutching an invisible drainpipe. And Hyacinth emitted an effeminate titter of amusement.

"*What?*" fired Colonel Brazier, spraying us with peanut shrapnel.

"Well endowed," explained Miss Pinch, her face flushing. Magnified by her lenses her pupils dilated like hot tar pools.

"Aha," the Captain declared with enlightenment. "Extra ballast, eh?"

"Met this Ghurkha once," the Colonel revealed. "Strapped his kukri to his middle wicket." Hyacinth giggled again, inclining her head to hear the graphic detail.

"Damn stupid place to keep it," the Captain offered.

The Colonel jerked his head. "*What?*"

"His kocki thing," Hyacinth explained.

"My God, woman," the Colonel barked, "where do you expect a man to keep it? Can hardly fit it in your top pocket, eh Claret?" And both dementias guffawed with bawdy military humour.

We returned to our places beside the alley, the landlord's dog curled sedately by the log fire, blissfully indifferent to the raucous, the passionate whooping, the rare moment of suspense as the player rolled his or her ball, the crashing of skittles, the raptures of joy or disappointment…

"Five, four, three, where are you?" came a voice from my radio, a friendly voice, her words a squawking clamour amid the tangle of fear and anticipation, my arms like pistons, my spade a jolting, thudding instrument of destruction as it glanced from wall to wall. "I'm in the cul-de-sac, where are you?"

I didn't reply. I had made it to the top, now staring with trepidation at the roof above my head. His weight a creaking, restless thing; a man disturbed. A man whose mind had long since tipped that fine balance of sanity and reason, now pacing fragile squares of terracotta like some imprisoned beast. Breaking tiles, snapping them with each burdened, mortal step.

"He's on the roof! He's on the roof!" I heard my lady cry, and then... *Thud-Thud-Thud* as he ran above me.

And a heavy, screaming silence followed in his wake.

Icarus was in flight, a beautiful swallow – his final gesture, his sanguine limbs of wax spread-eagled as he launched. *"Oh, my God! He's dived - he's dived!"* Diving... diving... his body crashing to that Tarmacadam sea – a yard from the bonnet of her car.

I rushed down two steps at a time, all fear abandoned. My redundant weapon now just a simple tool that lay upon the floor.

Icarus was there, a pathetic broken mess, that final spoor of life ebbing from him with each fragmented second filled, his gaping mouth, his twitching head - those images still haunting me long after he had gone. And I knew then that I knew nothing of this tormented man, this feral creature whom I had hunted like some rabid dog. I crouched down beside him, reaching for my handkerchief to place upon those cyaneous lips and breathe some life into this wretched, grotesque form that was once a man. But it was her words that checked me, her skin being several inches thicker than mine. "Cam, it's hardly worth it," she said, and perhaps she was right. But it doesn't stop me thinking of that night. The night poor Icarus took his life. I pray his soul's at rest...

"Nob-by, Nob-by, Nob-by…" the opposition enthused and Nobby arose from his chair, mug of real ale in one hand, skittles ball in the other. The women intrigued by his trousered assets – the men marvelling his skill as Nobby discharged his salvo like a well-slipped whippet, the meniscus of beer froth still unruffled as he slew the skittles with a vengeance. The roof was raised by their celebration.

In the commotion, however, in the distraction of their applauding, Colonel Brazier sneakily dropped a trail of pork scratchings, a spoor of condiment he laid upon the floor until he reached the log fire. One piece, just one piece of pork scratching was all he required to ignite the fuse, the remaining scrap he concealed in his large, plump hand.

I took position at the alley, aimed my master eye on the prime centre skittle and powered my ball with an amateur roll. All crashed save two that all but winced from their tenure, my second and third attempts failing to connect as Miss Pinch chalked up the score. The Misfits were behind by a generous whisker.

Hyacinth's score was even less impressive, and neither Arthur's nor George's volleys turned the tables. Then it became the turn of Captain Claret, his absence provoking a wealth of rabble dereliction from the Young Farmers. But it was as Claret emerged from the Gents that their whooping catcalls suddenly defused to ebullient laughter, rocking and cavorting with mirth and astonishment. The Captain had attached a redundant length of lead piping to his trouser belt, the pendulous article swinging crudely between his legs.

"Bloody 'ell!" one of the farmers rallied. "It's long John Wayne!" And it brought the house down, Claret swaggering to the alleyway, encumbered by his heavy appendage.

"Ballast!" he cried. "Ballast! That's the answer!" And he eyed up the target with the squint of an ancient mariner, facing the enemy side on, features locked in earnest, bracing himself, right arm primed and ready, the lead piping an elliptical counterbalance beneath his bowing legs. The audience falling to a hush, gripped by this lottery of fate, their liquid eyes and florid cheeks still damp from the strains of their sanguine merriment.

The Captain released his first torpedo.

Then a second....

Then a third that demolished all but one skittle, which danced, wobbled, and then sat stubbornly *in situ*.

"Bugger," the Captain declared.

Unknown to everyone, however, everyone that is except select members of Drizzlewick's secret junta, the Colonel had already set the time bomb, placing the last portion of pork scratching to the sleeping dog's nose. The nose had dutifully quivered, the heavy jowls drooling, the long flaccid tongue scooping up the tit-bit that it consumed with relish. The hound springing to it feet to seek out the thread of treats placed at its disposal.

Colonel Brazier, checking his wristwatch with military precision, promptly stood up and left the room. The Captain defeated, released his piping to exulted acclaim and retired to the bar. Nobby, the hero of the hour, again took his place at the skittles alley and, bolstered by beer glass and ball, prepared himself for his *coupe de grace*.

The landlord's dog, some ancient sheep ferret, having consumed the entire bag of roasted pigskins, began to strain and as Nobby's arm unwound, the dog suddenly released a liquid blast of wet fart. A fart that growled, frothed and bubbled like some volcanic slurry tank - ripping Nobby's concentration. The beer spilling dramatically as the ball slipped from his grip, ricocheting from the wall, two chairs and a table leg. And the door halted it - pressed urgently to its maximum egress.

Never, in the field of human rivalry had I known so few to cause so many to evacuate with such fervour. The stampeding patrons asphyxiated by the acid cloud of canine flatulence. And with aplomb, the dog simply returned to its place beside the fire to wallow in its putrid effluvium.

"So, why do you want to be a Ranger?"

It was a simple enough question. The interviewers watching with interest as I sat uncomfortably in my seat; I held a secret loathing for interviews.

"Because I have a keen interest in the countryside – conservation and rural issues, and because I enjoy dealing with the public."

A moment of silence lapsed between us as we sat across the table. Doug, the Head Ranger, rangy with short blonde hair, and Jeff, a Senior Ranger, tall and paunchy, top lip fringed by salt and pepper whiskers beneath a Roman nose. My toes had curled so tightly in my shoes they almost hurt.

"How are things going at university, are you enjoying it?" Jeff enquired beneath his moustache. As with many tall people, he sat awkwardly behind the confines of that desk like some folded crane fly.

"Yes, I'm doing very well," I told him, my toes uncurling as confidence and circulation gradually returned. "It took some getting used to, it's been a long time since I was last at school." I returned their smile, both of them sharing some sympathy with this mature student of countryside management. I doubted any of them would have traded places with me.

Neither of them held the qualification; they were stalwarts of the old National Park system where knowledge of Dartmoor and a love of the countryside were all that was required. Today, however, things were very different and although we roughly shared the same generation, we were worlds apart in our life experiences.

"So, you were a Met. policeman?" Doug asked, scanning through my curriculum vitae.

"Yes," I told them giving them a chance to read the detail, a summary of police skills and public service. To me it was a vast catalogue of experiences, some good, some bad - some simply too unpleasant to describe. Of course they knew nothing of this, only the stark facts before them in black and white, and a glimpse at the individual who spoke to them.

Another moment of silence followed; they seemed at a loss to know what to ask.

I had applied for this vacancy for a year as an Assistant Ranger with the Dartmoor National Park, advertised at university as a work experience module for Rummy students. I had managed to adapt to student life at two successive venues, but somehow this was different. To me this was my ultimate challenge, a chance to tame my police mould. Could this old leopard change his spots?

"So, you live within the National Park," Doug broke the silence. "Rented or owned?"

"Owned," I admitted with a hint of guilt. I was well aware of the issues concerning wealthy 'incomers' and the vernacular communities that were in decline, some too impoverished to afford the luxury of owning their own homes. The economic demand for such property was grossly inflated.

"What do you think about the decline in rural communities?" one of them asked, perhaps reading my mind.

"Well," I floundered. "The communities are changing for a variety of reasons, agriculture is enduring economic hardship at present, forcing some farms and businesses to collapse and move elsewhere, and this void is filled by incomers like me who are desperate to escape the urban crush."

"Back to nature," suggested Jeff.

"Yes, I suppose so."

"Incomers from places like London have brought some prosperity to Dartmoor because they're usually the only ones who can afford to live within a National Park," Doug took over, "but is that all they bring?"

"Some do have a chocolate box image," I explained. "The romantics who have little understanding of the rural way of life and find themselves in conflict with local custom and local expectations…" I hesitated for a moment as Jeff prepared to launch into another question. "And there's another incomer culture too," I went on, probably too much.

"There are those who feed their egos with rural snobbery. They like to identify with Conservation and rural life which they believe gives them status within the Idyll, as they see it. Many pander to nostalgia, resent change and cast scorn on all things new and unconventional," I smiled weakly. They seemed a little perplexed, even stunned by my analogy. "Sometimes, I believe we are even less sophisticated than our jellied ancestors," I added, but I wasn't convinced my answers were quite what they wanted to hear and I found my toes curling painfully once again.

"Yobbos," Jeff finally spouted. "We occasionally get the odd unsociable group on the moor – some can get quite nasty, how do you feel about that?"

"I doubt they could be any worse than those I dealt with in London," I told him.

"But Rangers are not policemen," he reminded me. "We have no powers to speak of other than the authority given by local by-laws, but we rarely prosecute. Nor do we want to prosecute," he revealed, "we prefer to gently persuade and advise the idiots out there who are mostly just ignorant of any harm they may be doing – lighting fires, feeding ponies, dropping litter…"

I had long suspected that my former training and experience could prove too overpowering for this new role, a more affable occupation being my goal. I had no desire to be permanently shackled to violence and dereliction – I'd had my fill of that. Instead, I was eager to employ a friendly face in this new environment. A face people could approach, a face the public would appreciate and not spit at.

"So this brings us to the next part of the test," Jeff informed me. "The other Rangers are outside laying on a little practical act if you like, to see how you perform."

Cumuli had gathered to watch the awaiting spectacle. The interview was over and I gazed with trepidation through the casement window, watching as Trendlecombe went about its daily chores.

Then I lifted my eyes unto the hills; the tors as bronze sentinels in an ancient Latin storm, sunbeams breaching clouds, spilling pools of honey on Elysian Fields of gold. 'I'm *not* a policeman,' I whispered to the sky, willing myself to resist my training and experience. I had a vague idea what would follow.

"Here's a radio set and a Ranger ID card." Jeff handed them to me. "You've been called to a group who have set up camp on restricted common land," he explained; a contrived situation that bore all the ingredients of Hendon, only this was Dartmoor and my role here considered less severe.

I was led to a group of boisterous men; their acting experience, I suspected, based on an ill-spent youth. There were three men in all. I absorbed the scene; one drunk and restless, one loud and excitable, and one chopping wood with a machete - he was my first priority. They had a tent, an open fire, loud music blasting from a cassette player.

"Hello gents," I smiled my friendly smile. "I'm the local Ranger…"

"What mate? Can't hear you!" The music a loud disturbance.

"Turn the music down, please!" I asked politely, with just a hint of a growl, the volume reduced as I kept a cautious eye on the machete, chopping, chopping with his back to me.

"It's an offence to play loud music," I pointed out, "it's an offence to camp here and it's an offence to light an open fire. Sorry, but you'll have to put it out."

"But we're going to cook some sausages," the macheted one objected, turning, the weapon a menacing article.

"Drop the blade, please," I warned him, but he didn't heed me, returning to his tinder. So I kicked the stones and earth to smother the fire.

"*Oi!*" The machete protested. "Don't do that, we've just got it going."

"Drop the blade and I'll explain why," I told him, but he was reluctant. "Put it on the ground, there's a good chap," I humoured him. Slowly, hesitantly, the machete was placed onto the grass and I promptly stood on it, denying him access.

Then Goliath staggered forward, very drunk and very aggressive, armed with a baseball bat. I had long since learnt that there is no reasoning with an intoxicated man, a policeman just does what he has to do without wasting any breath. But I wasn't a policeman –

God, give me strength!

"Put it down," I told him, and he wobbled up to me, a surly, malevolent character, his belly a vanguard to his thick arms and thick neck; the bat a powerful threat. I didn't retreat and he stepped into my face, a leering monolith. "Put it down," I said with forced tolerance. But a mist descended. A mist of blue that staved the sulcus throb and spurred the metalled heart to action - my arresting gears cranking in to place.

It happened so quickly, my reactions now in autodrive as I grabbed him, twisting – a crude *tia toshi*, a rusty attempt at judo that failed to throw. But it rocked him, exposing his arm for perhaps a second, and a second was all it took to yank him down to one knee. And as I sprang, my arms collected him, colliding, bowling him over to pin him to the ground. He was nicked!

But you're not a policeman! Some lucid neurone screamed too late.

Oh, shit!

"I'm so sorry!" I told Goliath, shaking as his belly quaked with mirth - force ten on the Richter scale. And I realised what a powerful chap he was.

"Hi," he said, "I'm Tim," extending me his beefy hand. I took it and we climbed to our feet. The act was over as the Rangers collapsed with florid hilarity, the performance infecting them, their faces streaming with tears of laughter.

"I'm so sorry, Tim," I apologised again and Jeff took me to one side. I knew I'd flunked it.

"You're not supposed to get involved," he told me.

"So what would a Ranger do?" I asked.

"You'd walk away," he said, "and call the police."

My boots stuck to the carpet, the blood clinging to the tread as I made my way through the hall and up the stairs. The fibres, thick with cruor, ripped and tore from my feet, some matted viscous membrane that had soaked the floor. Bloody finger trails macabre against the walls.

"Bastard!" The screams emanated from above. *"Bastard! Bastard!"*

"You okay, Bob?"

"Calm down – yes, Cam," my colleague told me, struggling with the victim, four puncture holes pissing blood. "Just keep an eye on the big guy." Bob pressing towels to the wounds to stem the flow.

"Fuck! Fuck! Fuck!"

"Keep still!"

"He stabbed me!" the victim cried. "He fucking stabbed me! *Bastard!"*

We had received a call on the radio. "A disturbance... male stabbed, ambulance called... male suspect armed with a knife... approach with caution."

It was Christmas Eve and doors and curtains were open wide, spilling amber rectangles to the night. Spinning blue wash flashes as we drew up outside. His silhouette so large he filled the doorway, eclipsing the hall light behind, the blade glinting in his hand.

How I dreaded working over Christmas. To many, Christmas is a wonderful celebration, an expression of love and generosity of spirit. However, there are others who are devoid of such love, their loneliness exacerbated, exposed to bitterness and spite. To them, Christmas was an odious sentiment.

I had long rejected my feeble police truncheon that was made of a light and flimsy wood. Throughout my service the only value it had served was to break a window to access a suicide and to hammer with frustration at an unyielding beer can one early Christmas hour.

So as I climbed from the car, I prepared to weave, duck, and wrestle with this mountain with the knife. Yet he spared me, holding it out. "Here you are, governor," he rasped. "I've just cut up the geezer inside." And I took it, the handle, blood warm and tacky, and handcuffed him to the railings before following my colleague into the house.

"It was the telly," the victim blubbed, naked in a bath of wine red water, frantically washing the blood that leaked from his arms, neck and shoulder. "I wanted to watch the film… *bastard!*"

"He didn't, I take it," Bob drawled, and the victim shook his head.

"He just walked up and…" he sobbed again, too distraught.

Recently released from prison, I suspect he was bored with the company and had simply earned his ticket back inside.

"Why did you do it?" I enquired of the alpine, and somewhere in that montane zone his craggy head inclined, grinning satanically.

"'Cos I fuckin' felt like it."

They were cute looking kids, their mother a placid English breed, although their father was feral, some beast of *Caprinae* that browsed Exmoor's fallow cliffs holding in check the shrubs and bramble tendrils that invaded its pastoral crowns. "30 for the nanny, m'handzum," the seller told us, their former owner, "and 10 for the kids."

They were going for a song and I wondered why, they were such a healthy and attractive trio, the kids skipping and butting playfully beside her, while mum chewed contentedly on hazel branches.

"You don't want a pair of geese, do you?" I enquired cautiously and the farmer's wife's eyes lit up with interest.

Hector and Hetty had been particularly belligerent the past few months; their eggs hadn't hatched, all their bluster in vain. But when they attacked a visiting family whose small children merely had to look at them to attract their wrath, I knew it was time for the geese to go. We had grown attached and didn't have the heart to eat them, so this seemed an opportunity too good to miss.

"Naw," said the farmer.

"How much?" asked his wife, and I scratched my head in thought.

"20," I decided.

"How old?"

"Two."

"Naw," objected the husband, "I don't want them blimmer things."

"Are the guzzies 'ealthy?"

"Yes, although she's been a bit off lay lately."

"Bah!" he lamented. "Donks (donkeys), goats, blummin guzzies – what's next?"

"We'll 'ave 'em," she told me confidently, her spouse turning his back in protest. "Take naw notice o'im," she said *en coulisse*. "E has his cows an' ruddy sheeps – an' I'm entitled to mine."

"I might be able to borrow a trailer," I considered, eyeing up the goats, "then we could swap animals…"

"Naw, don't bother wi' trailins," she told me. "Primrose is used to the car. I take her o'er to Trendlecombe after market day and she chooses her veg. from the stall."

A few days later, Primrose and her kids arrived in style at Tanglewood, chauffeur-driven in the estate boot of their car; Hector and Hetty patrolling their territory, hissing with menace.

"Yaw'll 'ave none o' that!" she wagged a finger at Hector and he cocked his head to give her an evil eye. And she stooped lower to stare at him, eyeball to eyeball until Hector finally buckled, lowering his head to the floor. "E's all beak an' trouzers is that'n," she declared, chuckling as the farmer surveyed my shed that contained, among other things, a redundant storage heater.

"Does he work?" he enquired.

"Yes, but we've had central heating installed so we don't need it anymore."

"Naw!" she protested.

"How much?" he asked, spurred on by her protest.

"20 quid," I said.

"Naw, you blimmer!"

"Done!"

"Maized az a brish stick!" (Daft as a brush!) she grumbled shaking her head with resignation. So the sale was agreed - three goats in exchange for two spiteful geese and a heater that weighed a ton.

Renaissance Ranger

The disco was loud at the Uni. bar, base and drums thumping from the walls, the ceiling, and the misted windows. Strobe lights flickered. Spotlights roamed the smoke filled air, glancing limbs, heads, and loose-clad breasts all bouncing in rhythm to some wild, frenzied dance. Even the beer glasses rattled and gyrated on the tabletops, a *courante* of liquored vessels.

Hippy reached out, plucked up his wandering drink and placed it back to its original position. Having rolled and licked a new reefer, he then lit it, sucking indulgently, squinting through its narcotic fog.

"Boris not here?" I enquired, almost screaming above the noise to make myself heard, and Hippy looked at me.

"Five quid!" his lips replied, offering me the joint.

"No!" I yelled, and emphasised the words again as if he were deaf. "Boris!" I exclaimed, sweeping back my hair and frowning as if to imitate some retarded Neanderthal. But Hippy just stared at me in a glazed hypnotic stupor.

"Oh, Boris!" Becky confirmed beside him, recognising my lampoon and she smiled wryly, pointing across the dance floor, a silhouette *en-masse* of convulsing figures. She read the puzzlement on my face and thrust out a salient arm to indicate the corner of the room.

My eyes trawled the shadows, the cavorting bodies, glimpsing a tangle of naked arms, legs and a pair of buttocks writhing against the wall. It was Boris, engrossed in copulation. His shaven head some buoy that bobbed against a lighthouse shore while limpet legs of female passion anchored his moon to her stern.

"He's busy!" Becky grinned. Todd fighting his way across the dance floor towards us and he handed us each a can of beer.

"Congratulations!" he yelled at me and Becky's features washed first by confusion, and then enlightenment.

"You got the job?" she screamed with delight, and I nodded.

"Bowled 'em over!" Todd exclaimed.

"Fantastic!" she gushed and planted a kiss on my cheek, an embossment of rings and studs, a rare show of affection.

"Start next week!" I told them. "How about you?"

"New Zealand!" Becky replied with excitement. "Three weeks time!"

"She'll be shagging the sheep farmer's son!" Todd bated her jocularly.

"Baaaaaa!" Becky effused, standing to pump the air with her hips.

We had spent a year together, a year attending lectures and writing assignments. We had examined quadrats, nitrates, woodland, even town and country planning acts. We had collated data and cited eminent authors from their books and specialist reports. Each of us had shared the highs and lows of academia and in a way it seemed sad we would be parting for a whole year, and yet exciting that many of us were embarking on adventures new.

"I'm stone walling!" Todd revealed. "And there's silage to cut!" Being a local man he had local commitments; he and his JCB and tractor skills were in great demand.

Hippy just stared at the window beside us, his eyes heavy with intoxication, watching beads of condensation – perhaps orang-utangs in liquid form.

"What about you, Hip?" I asked, drinking thirstily from my can.

"National Trust!" he revealed. "Data-basing Culm grasses!"

"Bollocks!" declared Becky. "Smokin' 'em more like!" And for the very first time we saw Hippy smile.

The disco blared from the elevated speakers, the lights mounted high on the scaffold that supported two incongruous machines. And they suddenly kicked in to action, spewing green foam that splattered all that danced nearby.

"Yeeeah!" Becky whooped excitedly, hurriedly stripping off her outer clothing before running, uninhibited, sports bra and knickers, into the cascade. Hordes followed her, a frenzy of half-naked party revellers; a spume of olive broth splattering their heads, their faces, their limbs and torsos. Boris still humping emphatically; immersed in avocado froth, he and his croaking girlfriend reminded me of a pair of mating frogs wallowing in their spawn.

"Cummon you lot!" Becky enthused, a dripping sculpture, Aphrodite *en* slime, bubbling lubricious lozenges from the ringlets in her nose. And we went with her, fully clothed, into the frolic, leaving Hippy with his dreamy faces on turgid melted glass.

Like some ailing victim of angina, London's arterial roads grew narrow in the capital's heart, my progress reduced to a palpitated beat. I sat at the wheel, waiting for the lights to change, waiting as my police radio trickled on channel one. There was a car in front of me, and a coach behind, buffered by terraced blocks as people walked and went about their tidal pith of life.

Then suddenly an angry face appeared in front of us. Then another and another, human walls of antipathy encroaching at the junction; a crowd to our right, a crowd to our left, one clad in the colours of Chelsea blue, the other in Arsenal red, and as one ragged wall advanced, the other retreated, then they would merge and clash with taunts of abuse, intent on violence.

It's odd, but I felt no fear despite the affray that was building before me. The emotion I felt was a sort of anger – a controlled, determined anger that had concentrated in my mind and limbs. I held the moral authority, and that power surged with a calm urgency as I climbed from my van, pressed my helmet to my head, and flicked on my van's revolving light, a pulse of Metropolitan hue. I approached that valley of wrath suffused by a profound grit to stop them and halt their shallow game of punch and kick. And as I entered into that corridor of hate, my vim and ire the cutting edge to a sword of conviction, I began to hunt for my first victim of arrest.

The river parted, the waves receding for a moment as I ran the length, snarled, and harried their intent. But I was only one, they realised, only one who bore the cloth of order, their many hands and feet now pressing to combat.

He was the first to rain blows on the opposition, and he was the first to feel my arm around his neck, a youth of 18 years whose desire for the spunk of battle had suddenly gone stale. He wore blue, so I began to chase a red to make the score more even as he dragged with me, his head imprisoned in my grip, locked in the strong limb of some growling and ardent warrior of nemesis - so suffused with anger I could have eaten them all!

But the reds eluded me, my trophy enough to quell their fighting stomachs and they ran, as clouds of startled rooks in flight.

The drivers and passengers of many halted cars and a coach full of sightseers had had a grandstand view of the drama as I marched my prisoner back to my van, their faces washed by awe as I locked up my quarry. And as I climbed into the driver's seat he broke down with self-pity.

"So, when are you going to beat me up?" he enquired pathetically and I looked at him and shook my head.

"You're the bloody oik," I told him. "Not me."

The epicentre of the Dartmoor National Park Authority emanated from a stately house that concealed a warren of corridors that lead to a variety of rooms, all occupied by assorted desks, computers and filing cabinets; workstations of the administrative staff. At its core swept a grand staircase that scaled the upper sanctum where the echelons dwelled within an emerald power - the naos of all things Dartmoor. Fields and manicured gardens surrounded the house and behind, less significantly, lay a courtyard with outbuildings where the Rangers, like soil fauna, were condemned to enjoy a lower status.

Tim, my burly wrestling partner from the interview greeted me, shaking me warmly by the hand, and I stepped into an arena of khaki clad men and women. They were solid, seasoned people of the moor; hands roughened by manual labour, sitting huddled around a large desk, their stout diaries abounding with extraneous memos that revealed a commitment of community liaisons, meetings, schedules and reports.

There were 10 in all. I had already met Doug and Jeff, and Tim introduced the rest, their names I clutched as dryad seeds borne on a summer's day. The girls smiled and nodded from their girly corner. The men grunted and grinned, and one said, "G'day."

A tall, wiry sort, he was a dark haired Australian who appeared as a native Devonian at first glance, his plumage betrayed by his kookaburra song.

"This is Oz."

"It's unlike you to be polite, Tim," gibed Oz.

"Oz, on a good day," Tim rallied.

"Matilda the rest of the time," Doug added.

"And what about Skippy, eh? Or Rolf, or Dame bloody Edna?" Oz lamented. "A man has feelings." And he gave me a sly wink.

"Do they have feelings down under?" Jeff enquired with sarcasm.

"So the rumour goes," Oz defended, "although many pommy traits are diluted by lager and sun."

Oz was a character. A former Ranger from New South Wales, his interest in his Devonian ancestry had influenced his decision to join the Dartmoor team for a couple of years' experience.

Doug read out the meeting's bulletin, assigned various Rangers to various jobs on the moor, swapped more banter, supplied me with a uniform, kit and a van, until he finally declared enough was enough and we all retired to the pub.

"You'll be helping Oz and Tim on their sectors," Doug informed me, pausing to stuff a fork full of plaice and chips into his mouth. "They're probably the busiest areas of them all, particularly during the silly season," he said, the silly season being from Easter to September when droves of holiday visitors flock to Dartmoor. "And they all have their peculiar problems."

"They're very peculiar Rangers," Freya quipped with a smile. An attractive, earthy girl she unleashed her flaxen hair from its allotment, tumbling locks of barley to her shoulders, the herbaceous border of a pretty face.

"Tim has difficulty with fly-tipping, poaching, and a few Plymouth thugs who enjoy wrecking parts of the moor in their cars at weekends. Oz has problems with visitor pressure on the honey pots (popular sites), campers, litter, fires, and masses of illegal parking... he spends half his time trying to appease the locals who frequently vent their spleens."

"But surely, half those are police problems," I suggested.

"You would think so," Jeff spoke up. "A few of the local police are good and help us out, but the rest just seem to want to leave us to it – but we don't have their powers."

"Nor their money," someone offered.

"Nor their grief," I added knowingly, yet I was beginning to understand their anxieties.

"But they seem to think Dartmoor is completely autonomous," Freya concluded from her lemonade and we fell quite for a moment as we pondered methodically on rolls and soup.

"Cameron?" Oz enquired above his cola froth, keen to change the subject. "After the Ranger interview, did you get those green strains out of your trousers?" But he didn't allow me time to answer. "Because Tim's still trying to get the brown ones out of his." And they all erupted into raucous laughter.

I followed him in my green national park van, parking up to leave my vehicle and join Oz and Joey in the front of his Land Rover, Joey a collie mongrel breed who stirred and snorted this renaissance Ranger that was me. And in silence we left the tarmac, Oz selecting four-wheel drive to ascend a pitted track.

We bounced and rattled along with the tools that were stacked behind us, an assortment of spades, handsaws, mattocks, a crow bar, jemmy, redundant MOD ammo boxes crammed with nails, a strimmer and a chainsaw, Joey suffering the ordeal by tractor with customary indifference. On the roof above our heads a huge grilled rack secured signs and posts and lumps of wood all lashed to the metal bars as adornments of a Ranger's hat. And with skill we traversed that boggy trail, clawing between gorse and hawthorn shrubs that scudded our flanks, scaling the vertex mantle, emerging to a col that embraced the moorland heights.

A panorama of copper granite heads beheld us, the misty forms of hills receding, melting to the argent line of sight. Beneath us, the valley banks were dressed with bracken, gorse and purpura heather; the brooks as milky threads that spilt and fed the River Kist below.

Oz stopped and turned off the engine, taking a moment to survey the view. The bracken nodding, the river a corybantic dance of light, the wind a choral elegy *mezzo voce* through his fluted metal crown. And he rolled up some benign string of tobacco, lit it and inhaled deeply.

"Welcome to my office," he said.

Lambs & Wolves

  A crowd had gathered. A host of anxious 'grockles' (holidaymakers) surrounded a foal that had lain undisturbed in the car park for several minutes. "Is it dead?" someone asked, prodding it with a sandled toe, and the foal's languid eye flickered. "It's dying," another suggested as a mare grazed nearby unaffected by the attention her offspring was stirring.

  It was a warm day, the sun illuminating this popular car park thronged by holiday visitors. They were a pleasant lot, keen to share their enthusiasm for the moor, for its wildlife and for the Dartmoor ponies that roamed the honey pots in search of treats.

  A group of these semi-feral ponies with babes was always an attractive sight. But they could be quite a pest, one and a half tons of horse-meat plundering the unwary family picnic. And yet many visitors indulged in the illegal act of feeding them, enticing these equine trouble spots to obstruct the narrow country roads and dine on crisps and cake that fouled their gut.

  They would haunt the river banks too, the grass frequently eroded by the many human feet, the fragile vegetation scorched by portable barbecues, trawling the discarded rubbish that is the bane of human ignorance and abuse. And here, in the car park, I watched as the crowd gathered and the traffic slowed to gloat.

  There was nothing wrong with the young animal, only minutes earlier I had noticed it suckling from its mum with rapturous content. The asphalt attracted them, a warm blanket of sun-blessed tar to lie against and doze away the infant tariff, indifferent to the liturgy of compassion that had pressed to watch.

So I went to them, clothed in my Ranger robes, and wormed a path through that European mix of men and women. The crowd parted and held their breath as I squatted low and heaved the chunky youngster to its feet.

It stood and shook and blinked an indignant glance before trotting off to join its mum, the crowd gasping with relief. "Oh, look," someone cooed. "Ja, ja," the Germans nodded as stern Dutch faces creased their talking holes and clapped.

"So, you're a horse whisperer now then?" Oli gibed from behind the counter. A cheerful sort with dark eyes and palmate ears, Oli was one of a small army of Information staff who manned the Park's buildings that served the enquiring public.

"Well, it did the trick," I explained, aware that this new Ranger assistant was still beneath the testing glass. "Anything reported?"

"Oz is busy with a school group this morning," Oli told me. "But he wants you to patrol the river as it's a warm day."

My 'beat' included a six mile section of the River Kist which followed a tortuous route through a deep gorge and wooded vale of outstanding scenery, a magnet for tourists.

To the north and south, a road had bridged its modest expanse, and car parks had swelled to accommodate the visitors who ventured little further than perhaps a few hundred yards along its banks, content to join the huddle and leave the wild waters to tumble mysteriously into seclusion. And there were the adventure seekers, the solo walkers, nature ramblers that yearned to taste the wilderness, to breach the canaille fog and embrace that mellow nook of solitude.

I spent an hour picking litter among groups that crowded the grassy banks, their children playing in the river. From the undergrowth nearby I dug out bottles, cans and carrier bags, tin foil barbecues and even a redundant tent. But worst of all were the disposable nappies, the shrubs and marsh grasses, once home to migrant birds, had transformed into rank lavatories.

"While you're there, can you take our rubbish?" a Torquay lady once enquired with a smile, and without a smile I accepted it. "They ought to put some bins here," she suggested. And I began to recognise Hyacinth's fears about the concept of an urban park.

"That would look nice," I told her rather tartly, "and the wildlife could pick over the spoils."

Her back was a broad and silent protest.

Resigned to collecting litter, filling skips by the sack full during the summer weeks, the Rangers and valuable volunteers tidied up these so called beauty spots. In an attempt at education, the Park had tried erecting signs sympathetic to the environment, advising visitors to take their refuse home. But many locals complained bitterly. "We don't like ugly signs," they argued, content to allow the debris to accumulate and grumble if the fairies were too slow.

I left my sacks of rubbish in my van and donned a rucksack, glad to venture the lonely miles along the river trail. The Kist roared beside me, churning against boulders, squeezing between granite clefts and fissures, spilling into pools of blue. Not a soul to meet, not a jot to care about as I removed my boots and dipped my feet into bracing waters; watching silver wash fritillary dance in flight, grey wagtails bob from rock to rock, the low skim of a dipper, the plop of a trout.

The banks grew steep and awkward as I climbed the old poacher's path beside the Kist, ascending rocky outcrops decorated by plumes of ferns, the roots of birch, sycamore and beech exposed by the torrents of a winter's spate.

Then the trail undulated. My brow pricked by sweat from the exertion as I squeezed both my rucksack and bulk beneath a mountain ash that leant drunkenly against its brother oak. The bark gnarled and rippled beneath my touch, the air damp and woody, mycelium earth and a stinkhorn's musk. Honeysuckled skeins dripping wild; arum jewels, celandine, spearwort and ransoms garlic. Heather scuffs and a bilberry's brush. And the incense of nicotine drifted sweet and faint.

I stopped to assess this incongruous spoor and looked down at the river's wooded vistas. I sensed a poacher and as I moved quietly down to the waters edge I spotted him, an elderly sort with a tatty coat and a tatty hat, stapled by flies and hooks, articles of an angler's bent. With pipe in mouth he was seated on a rock that spanned some rapids, water white as it churned the terrene soup, his rod poised, and the line adrift.

"Good morning," I announced, sitting along side him and his look was that of a startled fox. "Can I see your permit, please?"

"Permit?" he coughed on his pipe. "I... I don't have one."

"I'm afraid it's an offence to fish here without a permit," I warned him and extracted a notebook and pencil. "What's your name, please?"

For a moment he looked at me, enquiring eyes hedged by silver brows that revealed neither anger nor resentment, only intrigue.

"Leonard Wilson," he revealed and I scribbled it down while I briefly assessed him; save for a trace of a smoker's taint, his fingernails, like his teeth, were well groomed, the detail obscured by a day's swathe of beard mounted by a threadbare collar; his jacket embroidered by rustic stitching, and upon white downy locks a shabby cap resided, feathered fishhooks as squalid tenants. But he was a kindly man I concluded, whose genteel ambience seemed at odds with his roguish appearance. A lamb in wolf's clothing.

"And where do you live, Mr Wilson?"

For a moment he said nothing, courting mischief and humour that danced in eyes intellectual; his smile flashing an incisor of gold.

"Tell me," he said. "What would you do if I refused to tell you, or say gave you some cock and bull? What would you do, Mr…er?"

"Stone," I replied. In reality, I could do precious little; I didn't have the power and the crime was hardly a hanging offence, but I humoured him… "Well, I'd take down all the details of all the vehicles parked near access points to the river. I'd inform Oz of course and the National Park, and maybe contact the police to find out who you were."

"Good," he said, drawing smoke from his pipe with satisfaction, "and what about the riparian owner of this river, eh?" he enquired. "Don't you think he should be consulted?"

"Of course," I agreed, but the penny hadn't dropped. "I may need a statement from him to corroborate the evidence." And his laugh was a sudden explosion of air, rocking and clapping his hands with glee.

"My God," he coughed. "You're a wolf dressed as lamb. If I were a betting man I'd wager 20 pounds you are an ex-policeman from London." And he creased again with mirth as he read my enquiring glance. "I have you at a disadvantage, Mr Stone," he told me, wiping a tear of joy from his eye with his sleeve. "Oz has told me all about you, but you know, I've owned and fished this river for 32 years and I've never once been challenged – not once."

"They must know you," I suggested.

"Only close up," he argued. "I look like a ruffian, eh?" I nodded and Wilson smiled contentedly. "I'm glad they've chosen a real policeman to patrol the moor."

Saint James' Palace enjoyed a cloistered air of intimacy and regal graces, but perhaps the most imposing of its venues was Clarence House, residence of Her Royal Highness the Queen Mother.

"PC Stone," I introduced myself to the armed policeman at the door, revealing my police warrant card for inspection and he peered at me through his vista of moustache and helmet.

"So you've come to help us out for a while," he said. "We've been expecting you; we could do with the extra manpower."

The police control room was a complex affair, equipped with banks of alarm controls, monitors and armoury, manned by various white haired policemen who appeared to have been maturing in their seats for more than a century; Robert Peel their original Commissioner.

"Quickly get your self tooled up," I was told, "she may be back early." And I booked out a well-oiled revolver, replete with rubber grip, and filled the barrel; feeding my speed strip with several rounds of spare ammunition; strapping body armour to my chest.

Any security operative worth their salt knows that their charge is at their most vulnerable when they leave or return to their home or work place because it is predictable and thus exposed to attack. And the Queen Mum, elderly and popularly loved though she was, was no exception.

"All units stand-by, we're on the approach," the message was announced from HRH's mobile police escort and a moment of urgency gripped my colleagues as they took their stations.

"Cover the east drag," someone instructed, his finger thrusting at a wall map that displayed a topographical view of surrounding roads and premises. And I hurried to my new position, my police brain switching in to gear as I scanned the streets, the pedestrians, the passing cars, the houses - their roofs, their windows. Who was watching? Who was waiting? What spurious item had been abandoned in her path? What tree, what wall, what concrete bollard could offer cover, kneeling or prone, from which to return fire?

Her Royal Highness's car turned the corner, hotly followed by her armed escort. Both soldier and bearskin coming smartly to salute while I concentrated on the public. We could not relax for a moment until our charge was safely inside the building.

Her car drew to a halt. She alighted. She chatted. We watched the streets. We waited. We held our breath. Then finally, she went inside, the doors closing behind. And we all released a great sigh of relief.

But it wasn't until later, later as the staff relaxed into their routine, my police colleagues leaving me alone to watch over the control room while they took a break that I heard a polite knock at the backdoor. On opening it I discovered a very ordinary elderly woman wearing a very ordinary old coat and headscarf.

"Can I have the key to the garden?" HRH enquired.

"Of course you can, love," I told her, mistaking her for some patriarch housekeeper and having found the correct key I plucked the item from its place and handed it to her.

"I won't be very long," she assured.

"No rush," I said, "things seem to have gone quiet now she's back." And she smiled to herself, turned and left me.

Indeed, it wasn't until the security staff returned that HRH again knocked on the door.

"Oh, finished now, dear?" I effused, accepting the key from her.

"Yes, thank you," she replied with a smile in her eye.

"Mind the step."

It wasn't until I closed the door and replaced the key that I noticed my colleagues staring at me, aghast.

"What?" I enquired, to my chagrin.

Thank goodness The Tower was obsolete.

An empty crisp packet skimmed against the road surface, buffeting the curb before being swept up by the wind to slap against his calf.

He was an odd character, a stocky hunched sort, wearing a light blue overcoat. I watched from my rear view mirror as I waited for my children to emerge from the swimming pool, watching as he glanced about the length and breadth of Trendlecombe's high street. Waiting as people passed him by and as people left the shop. But when he extracted a pair of gloves from his pocket and placed them on, alarm bells sounded like klaxons in my suspicious mind. And the children chose to emerge just as he went in.

It was a dilemma many policemen would dread, the unwritten rule being that family and police duty you *never* mix.

"Wait in the car and don't move," I told them tersely, my blue mist on the brink of descent. And I left them, mouths open, faces perplexed, to cross the road.

"Where's he going?" David enquired.

"What's happening?" Edward asked, watching after me as I ran to the shop.

"Dad's on a mission," announced Anna.

"Great!" John said with glee.

I checked the cars parked nearby, all empty save for an elderly man - hardly getaway driver material, and I scanned the street and doorways for a possible lookout - nothing - just Trendlecombe's shoppers pondering their lives, expelling their quotidian chores.

A small corner shop sold sweets and greetings cards and pop. And as I entered and hovered beside the postcard carousel, I glimpsed my suspect approach the counter with a newspaper he had taken from the shelf.

I knew I was no longer a policeman, but a robbery was different and I had my citizen's power of arrest. Better I should defend my fellow neighbour than to submit to that jaundiced spectre of inertia and defeat, and I braced myself, the mist infusing my arresting mode as red leapt up to amber light.

"Hello, Brian," the shopkeeper greeted him with a smile, "and how are you today?"

"F... fine, thanks," Brian stammered, "b... bag o' lick sticks, please."

"Lollies?" she confirmed reaching for the jar and he nodded, placing his coins on the glass; exorcising my mist, amber light switching not to green but back to red.

"I thought for a moment he was going to attack you," I confessed to the shopkeeper when Brian had left.

"Who, Brian? Brian wouldn't hurt a fly," she told me. "He's just a bit simple, that's all."

"I saw him putting gloves on before he came in."

"Oh, he loves sweets but hates getting his hands sticky," she explained with a chuckle, and I felt like an oaf. "Are those yours?" she enquired, glancing over my shoulder, and I turned to see familiar young faces pressed to the window, four musketeers, one armed with a cricket bat, the others each with a wicket stick they had extracted from the boot of my car.

"You alright, dad?" their voices piped.

Pageants & Prejudice

"Okay, orange group, follow me!" I announced and a plethora of 10-year-old children swarmed beside me, all jubilant at their day's outing with the Dartmoor Rangers. To soften the formal image of my Ranger uniform I wore a jester's hat, replete with bells that the kids jangled at every opportunity.

"What's your name?" enquired Sophie, her name emblazoned on her badge.

"Cameron," I told her.

"Are you Scottish?"

"Scots, Welsh, English, oh, and a bit of Eskimo," I teased.

"Do you live in an igloo?" James piped.

"Only at Christmas," I joked, "when I have to feed Santa's reindeer." And they all sniggered, jumping up to take a swipe at my funny hat.

"Okay, lemons," came Oz's familiar twang behind us, "follow me to the dingly dell!" And a score of children, all clad in yellow t-shirts, swamped him like a celebrity, his wide brimmed Akubra at a jaunty angle.

"You're an Australian," one little boy observed.

"Stone the crows!" Oz exclaimed. "You're a bit of a smart Alec, I reckon."

Their schoolteachers accompanied the melee that snaked a path through the host farmer's fields, until we arrived at a glade in some woods. Freya was already there sitting serenely on a log, looking every bit a sylvan queen, her golden hair tamed and braided for the occasion, her group of children in busy attendance adorning her with daisies and dandelions; elfin sprites dressed in green.

"Right," Oz began, taking the lead, handing out a box full of coloured paper pieces cut from redundant table magazines. "I want you all to take one of these colours and try to match it with any leaf, beetle, bark or blade of grass..." and the children eagerly took their colours into the foliage. This was the first of a series of nature games which Oz clearly loved performing. He was a natural at entertaining them and they responded so positively that any ambiguous thoughts of ridicule I harboured soon evaporated. This was education at its best.

Then Freya stepped on to the floral stage; dendroid arms outstretched, the children in awe. "I'm the skeleton of a tree," she told them, "I keep the tree strong and upright, but I need some roots to anchor me and draw up food and water. Who will be my roots?"

Eager arms were thrust to the sky and several cherub faces lay down at Freya's feet. Then more came forward to form her bark, a protective layer of life, and more to act as her canopy of leaves, personified sugar factories to convert the light, absorb carbon from the air and yield oxygen by night. And their spirited choreography reminded me of a Native American proverb; Western history skewing them more towards their savagery rather than their affinity with nature:

'Tell me, and I shall forget.
Show me, and I may not remember.
Involve me, then I will understand'.

"Although there are 10 Rangers," Oz explained in a beer garden, after the day's event, "we each have our sectors each, with their different characters and problems, and often as not, we work on our own initiative, some days without seeing a soul."

"My sector, especially," Freya told me, sipping from a pint mug of lager," has fewer villages than most and with several thousand hectares of moorland heath and forest. Only in a few places am I lucky enough to find radio reception. It can be a very lonely job."

"You don't sound Devonian," I told her and she smiled, green irises flecked by an aurora of bronze.

"Half Scandinavian," she revealed, then raised her glass to drink.

"Only a few Rangers are Devonian," said Oz, munching on crisps.

"You have some Devon blood," she reminded Oz, wiping the froth from her mouth.

"Yeah, about enough to fill a gnat's wonker," said Oz with an antipodean's smirk. Suddenly, my foreign identity to this granite land seemed less significant.

"So what did you think of our childish games," Freya enquired more seriously, changing the subject.

"I thought they were very good," I told them honestly. "But had I not been there to experience just how much the kids get out of it, then I think I'd have been sceptical."

"Which is exactly the attitude of the other Rangers," she said. "Only they don't come and join in."

"What? Never?"

"Cameron, not all of us are confident speakers or entertainers," Oz told me. "Although we're a Ranger team, very often we each work in our different ways."

"But don't you share similar skills and interests?"

Freya shook her head. "We all love Dartmoor and we all preach from the same gospel, but our main problem is that many of the Park's senior staff are slow to change."

"Or don't want to change," I suggested. I was beginning to see a familiar pattern of stagnant management practice.

"If it ain't broke, then don't fix it." Oz imitated an old Devon adage, and I smiled. It always amused me to hear an incongruous stereotypical character utter vernacular words and expressions, rather like an Indian shopkeeper from Halifax speaking a potted version of Baltese-Yorkshire.

However, I knew that what I considered mild diversionary pleasure was antipathy and fear to some and not just speech, but skin-colour too…

"I ain't done nothing," he told me resentfully, a black Afro-Caribbean man sitting quietly in the beer garden enjoying his pint and I had no reason to disbelieve him; I had been called to a disturbance, not by the landlord, nor by his customers, but by the occupier of an extremely right wing political regional headquarters.

The word 'disturbance' is a peculiar thing in police terms. A universal expression, a disturbance describes practically anything from an argument in the street to a murder, and this incident had been so-labelled purely to provide a conduit of brevity and speed to the assigned police unit that was me. And I sat at the garden table opposite him, removing my hat to appear less imposing.

"All I know," I explained, "is that someone has called the police. You're the only guy in the front garden, so I'm just asking what's going on, that's all. I'm not accusing you of anything." I was taking pains to reassure him. Sometimes the tension between black and blue ran deep, and for a moment he said nothing, avoiding eye contact, supping his beer as his brow knitted, furrowed by the sapient plough of thought.

"Look mate," he finally told me in his London drawl. "I was born here, I live here, and I'm entitled to go where ever I want."

"Too right you are," I agreed. "So is this all about skin?" And for a moment he glanced at me, prising a fissure of hope.

"He called you," jerking his thumb at the grubby terraced building, just a brick's throw from the pub. "He's the one shouting his mouth off. Go talk to him." So I did.

A pale weasel character, short, thin, wearing cropped hair and boots, answered my knock on the door.

"Has he gone?" he enquired with a high pitched squeak.

"Has who gone?" I asked him.

"The nigger of course."

"I think we'd better go inside," I told him and he allowed me to step into his disturbed world of darkness and bigotry.

"I take it you called the police."

He nodded, nervous, squinting at the street through a venetian blind.

"He's still there, isn't he?"

"Who?" I pressed, although I knew perfectly well.

"That black shit in my pub, that's who!"

"What's he done?"

For a moment I thought he was about to erupt into some gyrating, vomit spewing demon, but disappointingly he simply depressed the record button on his tape recorder instead.

"Let's be clear, constable four three two," he growled, eyes bulging from hollow sockets. "I don't like blacks in my street, in my pub, or in my country." And I looked at him, struggling to scrape as much as a micron of respect for his pathetic affliction.

How I yearn for a world where black and white would not exist, just skins of tan that lived in harmony with moral and religious ideals of a common love and appreciation of our foreign neighbours and their foreign ways. As far as race, creed and identity are concerned, we simply coexist in ages dark and ignorant.

"We're talking about a *man* drinking in a pub," I told him, appealing for sanity and reason.

"We're talking about a nigger…" his voice quavered. "They're everywhere." And he scanned the street once more. He was genuinely afraid.

"I'm leaving now," I told him. "I've spoken with him. He's not doing any harm and he's just as entitled to drink there as you are."

"Aren't you going to arrest him? I want you to take him away!"

My anger at his callous insensitivity was stirring, and I struggled to suppress it. But suppress it I must.

"If you go out there and cause any more grief," I growled, "I shall arrest *you* for causing a breach of the peace. Do I make myself clear?"

He had based his fears on his own inadequacies; attaching his anxieties to a people he could not understand. Such as a people who had excelled at sport due to their inherently strong physique, a people who appeared aggressive and violent in the media coverage of riots, gang warfare and drugs. A people who shared a mixed racial culture and identity, a people once considered inferior by the historical arrogance of white supremacy. They were a people who dared to be different. They were a people who were proud to be black.

But he was not alone with his prejudice and his paranoia. I had met others too, mainly the vulnerable who peered at the world outside through a narrow vista of alarm and apprehension at the racial invasion, as they saw it. There were those who lamented the erosion of traditional ways and values, quaking from the incidents of a black rebellion that spat and clawed its enmity; resentful of authority and social injustices.

I climbed into my panda car, drove around the block and found a secluded alleyway to reverse into. I needed a minute, just a minute to compose myself and find sanctuary from the manic scream that is the policeman's lot. It had been a long evening, one of many and I glanced at the seat beside me, piled with crime reports and statements that had accumulated, all awaiting process at the station.

I was growing weary of the job, tired of running about, tired of trying to sort out other people's lives; many couldn't cope with their trials of life, and usually it was the police summoned when things were getting tough. The police wrestling to maintain a fair and even hand in a world that expect them to be perfect, expected them to be unaffected by the malignancies they faced.

Jaded by the ordeal of trying to patch up the public's problems and keep the lid on society's fragile peace, Life, I discovered, was rarely fair. Police work was a beleaguered industry, an unappreciated role, and one I increasingly found hard to enjoy. My police radio at times a constant heckle of succinct messages; 'unit to deal... burglary at... assault at... an RTA here... a disturbance there.'

Crime was rife in London. Assault, theft and burglary statistics were going through the roof, my colleagues and I spending almost our entire shifts visiting one victim after another, chasing our tails, trying to placate the distraught whose houses were wrecked; their property damaged, their possessions stolen.

The few witnesses that came forward described the suspects as white, but half of them were often identified as black. They usually came in cars, parked up in poorly lit roads and alleyways, and systematically tested doors and windows at the back of their target premises, sometimes hitting an entire street. Perhaps due to mistrust or sufferance, few of the reporting victims I met were black, the majority being white and they were often frightened and lonely people.

One frail and elderly man, I remember, lived a solitary existence within a hackneyed tangle of tenement flats. Deciding to resist the beck and call of my radio, I spent some time with him drinking tea with this old war veteran. And they came in all guises; an ancient barrow boy or two, a seamstress, a factory worker, even a Polish woman - a Jew who had escaped Hitler's tyranny. All had stories to tell and photographs to show; treasuring the ancient images of loved ones, cracked and worn by the caress of a thumb, by the tear stains of grief and compassion.

It made me realise that we all have a life story, a story of love and tragedy, and no more so than the elderly, irrespective of race or creed, those wrinkled vessels of time that are the most deserving of a patient and considerate ear.

The nights heralding Christmas were particularly hard. I remember almost an entire street had been burgled; the victims returning to their homes to discover presents stolen from beneath their pagan trees, the wrapping paper discarded about the floor. No hi-fi unit to listen to. No TV to watch. No video, no computer, no microwave. Their havens ransacked, the threads of love and joy defiled, denied the trinkets of life's simple pleasures, a door or a broken window to repair, the contents of their drawers and cupboards strewn about the rooms.

And where were the police when these crimes occurred?

Sometimes they were fortunate enough to notice the 'suspects' passing by, and sometimes they were shrewd enough to park up and hide and wait in heavily targeted areas. But often as not they were still trying to catch up with all the other victims who screamed 'foul.' There simply were not enough of us. There simply was not the time.

The job was depressing enough but without adequate manpower or support, the mood of my colleagues was dark and taught and the prospect of transferring to other, less troubled provinces of this mellow land was appealing. And from the Met, a rising exodus ensued.

Gnarled wooden beams embraced the ceiling, curios, china cats graced walls and window ledges, doilies, and napkins sat neatly on gingham tables. And an elderly couple entered the tea-room, found a table beside the window and sat down to peruse the menu. "Two toasted tea cakes, dear, and a pot of tea," the lady enquired, and Lucy scribbled down their order and retired behind the counter to prepare their meal.

A quaint little venue occupied a corner plot near Trendlecombe's market square, a grand position from which to see the town's summer carnival, and special constables were busy diverting traffic as stewards placed cones and bollards bearing lamps that flashed in rhythm to the music fare.

"Cummad'tadaTrecumcarnival!" the speakers blasted, a large Rastafarian bouncing behind the microphone, about as incongruous a sight as a rural winter bus service. "Cummad'tadaTrecumcarnival!" Two soul brothers strumming at electric guitars, and the drummer was white, his sticks dancing on taught fitted tubs. "Cummad'tadaTrecumcarnival!"

He was low on lyrics, I thought. His band mounted on the back of a lorry, draped in tarpaulin. "Come on down to the Trecum Carnvival," was his invitation to boot start the occasion, the word Trecum being easy speak for Trendlecome. And I watched with fascination as a steel band prepared themselves for their Mardi Gras. Trendlecombe stirring, long shirt-tailed children emerging from their homes, black locks hanging amid wide eyes and wide mouths, enthralled by this bizarre spectacle.

Then Daphne appeared, a batty female octogenarian endowed with limp hair, awry teeth and bad breath. She was a game old bird who enjoyed a good shopper's bargain when she saw one, possessing a penchant for haggling for just about everything. Including the gum in a child's mouth, so the fable went. And I noticed her from across the street as we both made our way to the little tea-room opposite.

"Mug o' chocky an' a slice," she told Lucy. Lucy keeping a generous buffer of space, protecting her shortbread fancies from Daphne's chronic oral zest.

"That'll be 60 pence, Daphne," she told her as Daphne pretended to be deaf, placing a few diminutive coppers against the glass counter. But Lucy was wise to her, not the first to fall victim to her incorrigible ways, nor the last. "I'm sorry, Daphne, but it's 60 pence or no mug of chocolate," she told her firmly. "But you can have your slice of bread and butter." The old woman hesitated for a moment. She loved her bread and butter, coating it liberally with sugar to dip into her mug to sup. And I stood behind her, waiting for an opportunity to speak to my wife.

"What she zayin'? 10 pence?" she turned and asked.

"60," I explained, and the ripple of excitement in her eye was plain to read. She enjoyed the challenge, rummaging in her purse for a few more coppers. "Going to the carnival, then, Daphne?" I attempted by way of distraction.

"Oh, dessay. I'll be begger'd if I doan't," she chuckled. "Eh, but I fancy tha' darky on the what'sits," she revealed with a corrosive grin. "Nice lookin' fella." And with that, she dropped half the contents of her wallet, spilling her week's pickings from Trendlecombe's pavements. Notes blue, brown and purple still wedged within their secret leather niches as coins fled to the shop floor, clattering and spinning in confusion. "Aw!" she cried plaintively.

Grovelling to the floor she resented my help as I plucked a few of the errant coins and handed them to her, and Daphne snatched them from my hand, glaring as if I was a thief. "Naw murdy maakin', maister," (no mischief), Mr she grumbled. And as she turned and retired to a vacant table, I deftly flicked a fifty pence coin I had concealed under my shoe, sliding it across the floor beneath the counter to land at Lucy's feet.

"I'll come by and pick you up in half an hour," I told Lucy and she smiled as I left her, the tinkle of the shop's doorbell drowned by the raucousness outside. And as I closed the door behind me, Rap throbbed in my ears.

"If you aint dumb, cum to Tre-e-cum, an' 'ave some serious fun, a' cum to Tre-e-cum! Get down on d'beat, 'ere in d'street! Be cool, be cool, be n'body's fool..!"

For 30 minutes I watched as four hundred faces bobbed, danced and cavorted to the carnival music. The steel band in full procession, closely followed by an assortment of tractors pulling trailers, adorned by crepe paper, tinsel and people in fancy dress. Their faces painted, toothy smiles engaged as mops of dark curly hair teased their eyes and ears; bare flesh exposed, shirts unbuttoned to the navel. And their women danced and cheered from the sidelines, a bouncing snake of rotund busts, a few as vibrant cantaloupes.

Daphne finally pushed aside her empty mug and plate, struggled to her feet and braced herself at the shop door. "Vury purty aitin'," (very pretty eating) she declared, and slipped out into the night. Trawling the crowded footways; foraging the cluttered streets.

Where Skylarks Sing

"Fox at 10 'o'clock," Lucy announced one early morning, just as I was getting dressed. The children had already left for the school bus and our ducks and chickens were free from their housing to range about.

Foxes are usually nocturnal, but sometimes I had seen unhealthy, mangy adults roam the daylight hours, along with expelled juveniles evicted from the den to make way for the next litter. Either sick or inexperienced, a day fox often resorted to desperate measures and our fowl were his intended fast-food breakfast.

Wearing only socks, underpants and a Ranger shirt, there was no time to lose as I freed my 12-bore from its secure hiding place, fed it two cartridges of five shot and dashed out of the back door to hide and wait beside the hen shed.

Five, then three fingers Lucy signalled from the top window. The fox now slinking in from the eight 'o'clock position just left of the house and I slipped off the safety catch and held my breath as chickens scratched and pecked the ground and ducks waddled and splashed contentedly in their water trough, oblivious to the impending threat; a postman's van now pulling up the track.

It had been the second time Ted the postman had caught me out. The first, one early morning when I was still in my pyjamas, poised like some crazy Inuit, bare-footed upon a lawn wrecked by moles, my garden spade aloft as I waited for the culprit to emerge from its pyramid of soil. "Morning Cameron!" he had greeted casually as if such a spectacle he considered far from odd.

But here was I, half-naked in my Ranger outfit and brandishing a gun, so I decided to move to protect both my modesty and reputation. Streaking across the garden with shirt-tail flapping, the Park's white pony emblem on the breast, shotgun in hand, Wallace & Grommet grinning madly from fleeting ankle socks, I sought refuge behind a generous granite rock.

"Morning Cameron!" Ted greeted once again, dropping mail in to our box.

"Oh, morning Ted," I answered sheepishly but just as he began to turn to return to his van, the fox suddenly chose to appear from a nearby bush. The fox just as surprised as me, my shotgun snatching up to blast it as it fled, through the fence and across the field. Yours truly vaulting after it, through the bracken, through the briar, crows scattering in flight as I forged a path, then knelt, aimed and fired my final cartridge. But that day the bushy tail escaped.

From the driveway Ted had watched this bizarre event with modest indifference, and he simply climbed into his van, turned and went, leaving me with my socks and shirt-tail soaked by dew, twin barrels smoking in the early morning bloom.

"Sorry I'm late," I apologised to Oz, climbing in to his Landrover beside him, Joey greeting me with an affectionate canine lick.

"No worries," he said. "Engine trouble?"

"Yeah," I nodded with ambivalence. "You could say that." And Oz aimed his vehicle to the moor, leaving my van beside the Kist.

"I bumped into Leonard Wilson the other day," I revealed, "thought he was poaching his own river." And Oz grinned. "Scruffy bloke, isn't he?"

"That's the fella," he said. "He tries to fool people every time with his various disguises, but everyone knows it's him, they just let him get on with it."

"A rural eccentric," I suggested.

"Oh, we've got plenty of those. But Mr Wilson's okay, gets a bit irate with the grockles now and then, though - thinks the Ranger Service is his own private police force."

We stopped beside the upper reaches of the Kist where a few remote properties clung to its craggy banks. Oz selected a long iron crowbar, a mattock and Devon spade from his tools in the back and together we ascended a well-worn path, scaling the rocky outcrops that looked down into the valley.

"These houses have had problems with localised flooding," Oz explained. "Not from the river, but from the run-off from these hills behind." Then he plunged his bar into the sediment beside us. "This was a ditch, believe it or not. It must be hundreds of years old, designed to catch the water and divert it away from the settlement and into the river. But with a bit of work, I'm sure we can restore it."

I examined the indentation that was flush with hog weed, nettles and elder, all rooted to the silted detritus with its layer of organic matter. Few would have noticed it unless someone had pointed it out as Oz had, and my eyes followed its course beside the path until it eventually passed into a concealed conduit beneath, before dropping away to an adjacent stream.

"I like a challenge," I told him.

That day consisted of digging out the entire ditch, shifting granite slabs that bridged the path and as I grunted and heaved the stones from their fixing I heard a gentle hiss. It was a harmless grass snake, over a metre in length; olive scales, black belly stripes and with a yellow collar.

"She's a beauty," Oz enthused, and we watched as it slithered away into the undergrowth.

There was something deeply satisfying about working out in the countryside and when we stopped for lunch we found a promontory rock from which to eat, and enjoy the view; shirts clinging with the sweat from our labours, boots and hands scuffed and filthy with soil, and we watched in silence as a buzzard sailed high above the valley in search of food.

"Rabbits," uttered Oz.

"Where?" I enquired, and he smiled.

"His tucker," Oz described and he reached out to pluck up a pelt he found discarded on the ground, the indigestible remains of the bird's regurgitated meal, pulling it apart to reveal hair and compressed bone. "This is rabbit," he identified. "She eats mice and birds too, but rabbits are her main diet which might explain why their numbers are growing." And I gave him an enquiring glance. "Myxomatosis," he explained. "Back in the Sixties, the rabbit disease was introduced to kill off the rabbit population that threatened the field crops – they've had big problems back home too." He paused to press the remains of his sandwich into his mouth with grubby fingers, chewing liberally, undeterred by such towny qualms as hygiene. "But what no-one realised," he continued with muffled words, "is how much negative affect that food chain had on other wildlife. The buzzard population declined dramatically as the rabbits pegged it."

"But rabbits seem to be doing okay now," I offered.

"Sure, and the buzzards are increasing, until the next government dork decides to play God and hits the countryside with something else."

I nodded with agreement, sharing his reservations.

"I'm not a great fan of royalty, "Oz told me, "but the only one who seems to know what he's talking about is Charlie. I know many locals here think a lot of him."

"Yes, I suppose the problem with any government is that it rarely sees beyond its four or five years in public office," I told him.

"Yeah, that's one thing," Oz confirmed, cutting off a piece of apple with a knife to compliment his cheese, "the other's that most of them haven't got a clue about life beyond their artificial world of fast cars and fast-food. And with that he wandered over to the damp wood, browsed the floor and returned munching sorrel leaves and wild garlic. "Good bush tucker," he said.

We finished the ditch that afternoon and as we washed our digging tools in the stream, I glanced with pride at its revealed contours and new culvert bridge, watching as we reopened the path to allow to the public to enjoy their walk with unassuming ease. And I was keen to see it over winter, doing its job by diverting the watershed away from local homes.

"Tomorrow, I'm at a meeting," Oz told me, reaching for a map, "so if the weather's good I'd like you to walk the high moor and check the access points of a New Take (new margin of agricultural land). Take a few nails with you," he advised, "and something to hit them with."

The next day I approached the high moor with a sanguine heart, the summer warm and radiant against my arms and face, and my dogs barked excitedly as I strapped on my boots, selected a few tools from my van, and donned my rucksack. Just me and the moor and my three dogs as we set off along a compass bearing o'er broad heaths and vermian hills; tormentil, sedge and saxifrage a mat of crewel beneath my tread, then downy wisps of cotton grass and mollinia's rustled thatch.

The high moor was awash with bird song; a cantabile of volant skylarks, a cuckoo resounding, chased and harried by their wrath to dip and bob in flight, settling against those dry stone walls then shouting out to mock. Wheatears, meadow pipits, and a gnarled and injured post, Merlin's perch with copper worm, too slow to wrest its mortal coils from such a brutal taloned clasp.

I repaired ladder stiles and gates and finger posts, fasting steps and treads and wooden rails as the sun annealed my brow, my dogs panting, crickets rasping melodies while crane-flies droned and formica ants assailed the shrubs to prom their *paso doble*.

The heat shimmered in the verdant summer air, smells of pollen grasses imbued with heather, the coconut scent of gorse blossom, and the must of peat, reed and rush that clothed the banks of waters sparkling and ebullient. And my dogs crashed into its cooling depths as I undressed and gasped, immersing into its embracing gush to wallow humble and content, my mind subdued, Assama's balm expelling poignant memories that fester in their tomb...

"Get your fucking hands off of me!" a girl complained to her captor, a burly constable clutching a bag of stolen vodka in one hand, while restraining her with the other. "Turns you on, does it?"

"Look out, Tif." Another young woman, her partner in crime, giggled beside her. "'E might get 'is truncheon out." And her laugh was as loud as sluiced effluent.

The police station charge room was full of prisoners and police, the custody sergeant trying desperately to keep his head above the rising tide of work.

"You're havin' a laugh, aincha?" a man protested from one corner, a policewoman holding him firmly by the arm.

"What's he in for?" the sergeant enquired briefly.

"Assault," she announced. "He likes beating up women."

"An' I'll fuckin' beat you..." But he didn't finish, she had forced him down to the ground, his arm now occupying some unusual angle beside his ear.

"Shut-the fuck-up!" she snarled. And he did.

My prisoner stood beside me, leaning heavily against the wall, a driver who had failed the breath test. We were in a queue and we were the last, and he watched in stunned silence as the sergeant recorded the shoplifters' booty, three carrier bags full of alcohol stolen from a local supermarket. Each item he placed and sealed in a clear plastic bag, numbered, and locked away to be returned to their rightful owner.

"Right," the sergeant sighed, reaching for another charge sheet to process the next prisoner, the women escorted to separate cells. "Photographs, fingerprints, antecedents, statements, copies for court, CRO (criminal records) and a Please Allow (bail enquiry)," he reminded their young arresting officer.

Then it happened, suddenly and violently.

The building shook; the tremors quaking a subterraneous path from the seat of the explosion, barely a mile away - a mile from scenes of mayhem, carnage and destruction.

The wreckage lay smouldering, strewn across the road, the pavement, the shop windows broken, shards dripping. Entrails scattered about the tarmac. A head embedded in a tree. Half a torso deposited in the gutter on its back.

Casualties lay on the ground, hair singed by the heat of the blast, faces scorched and peeled like rubber masks - a man staggering blindly; a woman cradling a shoe in her arms - her foot still in it, sitting within Stygian creeks of blood.

This terrorist bomb was just one of many in those troubled times, scenes that had spared me for I was there only hours earlier, although then the device had not been left.

Every minute of the day and night policemen and women were searching abandoned boxes and bags, cars and containers that appeared out of place. Searching with a nonchalant air of fate as they examined and assessed, such was the overwhelming number of suspect devices that plagued them, they often could not afford the luxury of time to call on expert advice. And from the station corridors and stairs we heard the urgent thump of feet as the few embarked on their siren wail of duty.

"Jesus Christ!" my prisoner exclaimed. "Why you bothering with me? You should be out there catching those bastards."

"He can't leave until he's finished with you," the sergeant told him bluntly. "In any case, he's already caught one. More lives are wrecked by dodgy driving than any terrorist bomb."

Harsh though his remarks may seem, in many ways I believe he was right.

Of Beasts & Common Men

The job in question was a wooden stile. I had the previous experience of dismantling and building one with Oz elsewhere on the moor only weeks before, although doing it on my own without his guiding eye would be something of a challenge. So I gathered the materials for the job from my van and set off along the fields.

About a mile I carried the wooden posts and rails, making a return trip to collect tools and a Ranger's friend: a two-litre bottle of water. It was thirsty work; digging out the old rotten posts that had lain undisturbed for some twenty years.

Using the long iron crowbar to prise out the rock, then burying the posts, leaving two thirds of their height above ground on which to attach the rails and a footstep; ramming layers of rock then earth with the blunt mushroom end of the bar to firm their foundation.

"Everything tha' comes out, must go back in." Mr McVitee's tartan words came flooding back from agricultural college; an epoch that now seemed a world away.

Some bullocks came to visit me; three South Devon Reds, their broad satin noses testing the air as I worked. They were a docile breed, watching with big bovine eyes, flinching as I hammered home the nails. And their tails swished as they encroached closer to examine my labours, delicately nuzzling my shirt and snorting with curiosity.

"Look here, moomins," I told them, "go and find something green to eat." And they stared and shivered the flies that tormented them as I patted and brushed their noses with my hand. Sleepy-eyed with contentment, one evacuated a giant stream of pee. "Okay," I told them, disgruntled, "now you're getting too familiar." And I clapped my hands and pushed their shoulders until they scampered a short distance, only to repeat the performance again and again.

Collecting my equipment, I climbed over the fence to escape their attention, and it foiled them as I set about completing the job from the other side. And as I knocked home the last nail, dug a deep hole and firmed in a new fingerpost, I suddenly became aware of the subtle ripping of grass close by. A flock of sheep, Suffolks and Devon Short Wools, were grazing happily behind me, creeping closer and closer to inspect their visitor.

"Your animals are very friendly," I told Mrs Crowe when I returned to my van.

"'Cos I look after 'em, see," she smiled. She was a kindly sort. "Always 'ave, an' always will. But chickens," she went on, "now chickens are anuver thing… chickens niver fight," she announced, a Welsummer hen dangling lifeless from her hand. "No, no they don't. They niver stand up for the'selves…" Mrs Crowe was the farmer's wife, and when she got on to a subject she never let go. "No, they niver fight, do chickens…"

"Was it a fox?" I enquired by way of conversation, and she looked at me.

"Naw," she said as if chewing nettle, "blummin' foxes would 'ave torn 'er tay bits." But she offered no easy alternative.

"Ate something bad, perhaps," I attempted.

"Nowt bad to ate, 'ere," she corrected. "No, no chickens niver stand up for the'selves. No, no they niver fight do chickens…"

And on leaving Mrs Crowe alone to ponder the mystery of her hen's demise, I glanced into my mirror as I drove away, seeing her fowl emerge from their hiding places to clamber lovingly about her feet.

The sky grew dark, the clouds casting malevolent shadows against the land. Tree limbs tossed and creaked in the wind as my wipers swept rain and hail in broad arcs, my van forging a path through the clinging blackness; headlights painting the granite walls that were scrolled with ivy, hedge banks knotted by hazel and oak, and the fields were yielding their earthen waters as the lanes ran thick with Ceres's blood.

I turned into the narrow track that led to Studs farm and saw Oz's Land Rover, along with other assorted vehicles, and farm dogs barked excitedly as I arrived, sniffing my legs as I entered inside. It was a big old farmhouse, a little rundown - granite walls with small windows, worm-eaten doors and low oak timbers that ribbed the yellowed ceilings. And the taint of damp dogs and tobacco pervaded the air as I removed my boots and padded along the corridor in my socks towards the murmur of conversation.

"60 cattle," I heard someone affirm in a high pitched squeak. "60 cattle I'm allowed on Kist Common, an' it don't say when I can put 'em out."

"I put 'undred yaws (yews) on o'er winter," someone else added.

"Trouble is that cattle do the most damage over winter," I recognised Oz's special brand of patois, "poaching the wet ground where they gather to eat the hay you feed them."

I knocked politely on the door and entered, and the conversation stopped dead. Some 12 rustic faces stared at me, all huddled in the room, all hesitant, all reserved, all suspicious of this outsider of whom some knew very little, and most had never met.

"Hello," I smiled and found an empty seat.

"This is Cameron," Oz introduced me, "he's my batman."

"Aw, cricket, eh?" one enquired mistakenly.

"No, not crisket," another corrected, "perhaps 'e sees them bats, does 'e?" Flapping his hands to emphasise the point.

"Blummin' daft filum," someone complained. "Mind, catwomen was a bit'o a'right," and he pursed his stubble lips to grimace some leering gesture.

"No, no you don't get it," Oz corrected them. "He's my assistant."

And they frowned with confusion.

"Whyz you callin' him 'Batman', then?"

"Aw, like whatisname..?" an old farmer squinted his eyes in concentration.

"Aye, them flying machinations…"

"First World War jobs," another concluded and they all nodded agreement.

"One o' my aunt-sister's in Sicily," piped an old agrarian beside me. The connection with bats or assistance I grasped, as fog on Great Mis Tor.

"That's nice," I told him, imagining him with some Mafioso connection. "Do you see her much?"

"Who?"

"Your aunt's sister?"

And he slapped his knee with mirth, his smile gaping like split shoe leather.

"Naw, nort aunt's sister – aunt-sister (ancestor)."

And they all guffawed in rich Devonian hilarity.

"We've been here an hour," Oz whispered. "This meeting's supposed to be about getting an agreement to reduce the winter stock on the Common, but they keep wandering off the subject. It's been murder."

"Waz he one of 'em Barons, then?"

"No," the old boy told them vacantly. "No I don't think so."

"Our Nell's been o'er to Ibeeza (Ibiza)."

"Is tha' in Sicily?"

"Naw, it wasn't Sicily..." the stalwart gathered his wits. "Esher! That's where 'e be, Esher."

"Esher's the capital of Sicily, isn't it?"

"Naw..." another replied. "It's Ibeeza."

"Surrey," I told them. They mistook it for 'Sorry?'

"Ibeeza!"

"No, Esher is a small town in Surrey," I corrected. I thought I was going mad. "You know? In England." And they all fell silent like sulking schoolboys. I had spoiled their fun.

"Can we get on with the meeting?" Oz enquired, and they shuffled in their seats. "At the moment three of you have Belted Galaway heifers on the Common over winter," and a few nodded. "And you have sheep in in-by land in your fields." They nodded again. "Why not swap them over with Devon Reds and Scotties (Scottish black face sheep)."

"Reds aren't hardy enough," someone objected.

"Have Reds in the summer and Scotties over winter – they'll do less damage."

"Wind an' rain does more damage than a few 'undred Galaways. P'raps you should be spakin' to someone else," and he jabbed his thumb heavenward.

"Aye, an' can the National Park arrange a good silage week while you're about it?" And they all chuckled.

"Natural erosion we accept," Oz tried to keep the subject rolling, "but damage caused by human ignorance is something we can all avoid." Encouragingly, a couple of them nodded consent, but those that didn't were less impressed.

"Who the 'ell are you to tell us what's best," growled a recalcitrant. "An' a bloody Australian at that. We've worked 'ere on Dartmoor all our lives, an' you come along wi' your fancy ideas from the bloody National Park. Bloody waste o' time the lot of 'em."

"How's your ESA money, Jack?" Oz reminded him, the whole of Dartmoor designated as an Environmentally Sensitive Area, the European Union and the government funding those who agreed to farm the land sympathetically. "Enjoying your other subsidies, too?" And Jack fell silent, as they all did. It was a sad fact that upland farming was dependent on government handouts - perhaps too dependent.

"Despite our differences, I know you care as much about the moor as the National Park," Oz told them. "We just have to try to get along and work together, not against each other. All I'm asking is that you think about it, that's all."

A moment of reservation covered them like a blanket. Oz wrote notes as they shuffled in their seats, supped dregs of cold tea from idle cups, lit pipes and cigarettes, while the fire in the grate hissed and smoked along with them for rapport.

"Funny thing, really," the elder spoke up, breaking the silence. "Dartmoor's nort but a load o' auld rocks an' grass."

"An' brimbles (brambles)."

"An' auld hedges."

"An' wurtles 'n' auld twine (bilberries and old bale twine they use as temporary bindings to repair gates and fences), I reckon."

And they all laughed. Their mood had changed and they were jovial once again.

"Will they reduce their stock on the Common?" I asked Oz after the meeting.

"Some might, but I doubt they all will," he told me. "Farmers are a very hardy breed and fiercely independent. They like the freedom to run their business as they like. Some thrive on schemes and handouts, but many resent advice or financial help, even when they have no choice - sometimes biting the hand that feeds them. But it's a sad fact that without government subsidies many small farms would perish, and we'd end up with fewer farms, just bigger ones."

"The big farms of the lowlands seem to be doing well," I reflected.

"They are," Oz agreed, "but bigger doesn't mean better. The countryside isn't just about fields, woods, and streams. It's about community, and the way we manage, work, and live in a land people love so much. People are passionate about their way of life here and feel threatened by town and city folk that treat it as holiday resort. Reminds me a bit like the ranches back home in the Territories, some are so remote they lose track, almost turning aboriginal."

"Seems to me that those who live in the country are more dependent on their neighbours for kinship, and work harder at it," I concluded. "They enjoy the peace and the seclusion and feel privileged to be part of the natural world around them."

Oz fell silent for a moment, and then looked at me.

"You know, for a John (policeman), you're not such a dill as I thought," he told me.

Praise indeed.

Tongues of flame hurled into the night, arcing, spinning as raining meteors of fury, hitting the ground, spewing venom cocktails against our legs and feet. Wreckage aflame, our helmets of blue painted red. Our pressing shields some plastic barrier wall, interlocked and segmented. The many vicious screams and jeers. The savage silhouettes of faces corrupted by malice, spurred by the siren clamour of revolt. The glistening of knives, blades and machetes as they lanced, cleaved, and chopped. The throw of rocks; the hurl of masonry hitting colleagues, our forms crumpled by fear, by exhaustion and by lesions of both agony and hate.

Javelins like needles, launching at our walls, smashing through plastic, bone and sinew. "Man down! Man down!" Gloved hands grasping the limbs of their injured; dragging them from the plinth of antipathy. Blood spilling, impaled by Acheron's curse of terror, the stigmata of battle...

"Cup of tea beside your bed, Cam."

...One shield phalanx stormed a concrete stairway that lead to balconies of flats that rained rocks and bottles on our heads. And a dozen rioters confronted them, all armed with knives and hatchets that rained and hammered against their aegis wall, reaching over, hacking at helmet heads, slicing visor faces, cutting arms and shoulders. And the wall retreated, the rioters consumed by passions diabolic...

I felt Lucy's soft mouth press my cheek. "And she awoke the sleeping prince with a kiss."

...Shotguns blasting, piercing the tragedy of our chaos enmeshed. "Armed assistance! We need urgent armed assistance!" Armed units were there on stand-by, waiting for the order to deploy, but their plea went unheeded by an arrogance superior. "We need help here! *We need some fucking help!*" Too late, we had lost; his head hacked to death, and that impotence we all suffered with such embittered disgust...

"Your tea's getting cold."

...Anger, pain and despair lay as sedimentary layers of rock for each afflicted year of service, and I was not alone. Each man and woman who wears the cloth of blue bares the public's callous burden like some enormous cross of lead. Reflections of their own antipathy, the police are targets to their enduring spite...

"Dad, it's time to get up." Curtains were drawn and sunlight streamed through the window, my eyes adjusting to focus on familiar objects. Edward was smiling angelically beside me, his blonde head illuminated by an aureole of morning hue. They all crowded around my bed as I blinked and stared at them. They were getting taller, I thought, their faces maturing. They were fast growing up.

"Happy birthday, dad," they said, and placed gift-wrapped parcels beside me. I removed their paper coverings, aftershave, a shirt and a bottle of wine. And a box that contained a large brass handbell.

"Thought it might come in handy," said David.

I thanked them all and later placed the bell in the dining room where it lived within easy reach to ring loud and strong through an open window to announce lunch or when their friends called on the telephone. And the children would come from woods, fields, and riverbanks to muster at our home.

It had other uses too, tethered around Primrose's neck as she browsed the hedgerows while Anna and John took her offspring for a walk along a bridle path, their strong heads straining at their leashes to reach some extra tasty morsel that teased their tawny snouts.

Then one night when we were away, a badger clawed his way through the side of the duck house and helped himself to a downy meal. I repaired the hole and moved the few survivors closer to the house to occupy a shed, where foxes and even mink, dug and worried the slatted walls and door. From 12 fat and healthy fowl they had reduced to four in a matter of days and I declared war on their assailants.

The bell hung upon a nail above my bedroom window, a tocsin string attached to the handle, spanning the midnight yawn of darkness. And it bowed above grass, shrub, and fence to the carrion of a duck, the macabre remains of the predator's meal I had left suspended from the branch of a tree.

For an hour or more the bell was silent as I tested the field with a searchlight, a torch taped beneath the barrel of my gun; the weapon an answer to my anthropocentric call. And I waited... and waited... then leapt from my seat at its sudden toll.

Dashing from the house I ran through the shadows, slipping on dewy grass as clouds scuffed a sickle moon. And the bell clamoured in protest, the fox tugging at the carcass, dropping it as my light caught his eyes, burning like Orcus lanterns in the night.

And the crack of my shotgun snuffed out his feral *vulpes* life.

Yogi's Smile

A bead of sweat trickled from my brow, running some course, some saline path along my nose, dripping to my hand below - the hand that held the revolver, finger alongside the trigger, supporting hand cradled beneath. And I held my breath, listening, listening for some sound, some spoor of movement. But for a moment, there was nothing. And the corridor beckoned long and malevolent.

Dave had pressed his back to mine, his revolver covering the space behind me; mine covering the yawning hole that was the tunnel. And we crouched, walking sideways as crabs back to back.

In almost total darkness we had entered, extinguishing the light to avoid our silhouette as we searched for the gunmen who had escaped within. We wore body armour, our bulky forms as beetles as we stole through that dim labyrinth. We had called for back-up and it would find our empty car abandoned outside as we explored the depths in the heat of the moment, the gunfire drawing us to the scene of the crime.

A figure before me! Armed with a rifle! My arms pumping out with my revolver. "Armed police!"

As I ignited a dual spasm of light - two faces emerging alongside and I swivelled and knelt, the fire from our guns crashing all around; the stench of cordite filling the air.

"Reloading," Dave told me, ejecting hot casing to the ground and I glanced to my left. A suspect emerging at the door and I shot him - twice, a double tap, punching holes – one through his chest the other struck his neck.

"Full," he told me, springing to his feet. It was my turn.

"Reloading," I answered and rained metal husks to the floor. Always his body in contact, a leg or a hip, without it we might have lost communication and simply shot at each other in the chaos of the dark. "Full," I announced, my revolver replenished, and by a recess, two feet betrayed its owner's presence, crouched and menacing. "You, by the wall! Put the gun down! Come out with your hands up!"

No answer, so I dived prone, aimed my master eye on the target and squeezed one fatal blast.

"Nice work," complimented the police firearms instructor as we blinked hard in the wash of suspended light; our weapons emptied and proven safe. "You hit all targets, including the guy armed with an umbrella." And I examined the life size wooden cut-out, plastered with patched-out bullet holes. I wasn't the only one to have mistaken him for an armed suspect. There was usually at least one ambiguous target among a host of hostiles, and even in broadest daylight it was sometimes difficult to discern friend from foe.

"Can't you shoot the gun out of their hand like they do in the movies?" one group of builders once enquired as I left the police range. "Can't you aim for their arms or legs?" another suggested. Their reality on life they based on myth.

"Wounded suspects are just as dangerous," I advised them. Well intentioned though they were, they were ignorant of the high degree of skill it took simply to hit the biggest area of the target – the chest; often a millisecond decision to assess the extent of the threat. And if the target moved, which it frequently did, it was harder to even hit it at all.

A policeman's duty to protect often proves as profound a tent of clay as his regret. The public was my charge, my responsibility and I had no qualms about the role of defending them; stopping those who wanted to destroy, intent on greed and power, their hearts as frigid arctic wastes, their minds as arid pits. Armed officers deal with confrontation in their own private way. For me, I imagined the mothers, fathers, sons or daughters of the intended victims were with me, each pleading with me to protect their loved one from immediate harm. Sure, the one who wields the gun has relatives too, but the wielder's paltry value for the lives of others quickly reduced my sympathy to nil. Indeed, the suicide bombers that manifested later on, beyond my career horizon, was a new concept to London and a new challenge to my future armed colleagues who had little idea how to 'stop' a mobile human bomb. Indeed, who did? Always the police marksman bears the brunt of public anxiety – *'Why did you shoot him?'* then *'Why didn't you shoot him?'* if the police appeared too slow. It was an unforgiving task marred by public ambivalence.

Not all policemen were reconciled to the use of firearms. British policemen seldom are. Indeed, some colleagues scorned those such as me who possessed the skill, dismissing us as gung-ho cowboys. Only an armed incident – a robbery, a fatal stabbing, or a terrorist attack would focus their resolve.

One passing police car, I remember, was particularly keen to employ my protection as I was relieved one night from guarding a principle against the threat by the Provisional IRA. More bombs had rocked the streets of London, and we trawled the roads and subways for the suspects, but found none. Then the next day, the event forgotten, my gun and I would become the jocular butt of their ridicule once again.

"This is the blunt end," I deliberated, holding up a trench spade for all to see. "This is the sharp end," pointing to the blade, then I replaced it to the display on the ground by my feet and selected an iron bar. "Anyone know what this is?" A few shook their heads, the rest of the group looking on in stony silence. They were office people, administrators, clerks, and secretaries, and the prospect of physical labour made their faces pale with fright. "This is a crowbar, heavy and strong and useful for prising out stubborn rocks. Blunt end… sharp end." And I drove it firmly into the ground to demonstrate. "Give it a little wiggle," I eased the bar back and forth, then wiggled my hips in an attempt at humour, but their faces were bland. "Then prise against any resisting rock. If it's too big, then you'll have to probe the bar around the ground to find a suitable soft bit… Okay, if you'd all like to select a 'weapon' and carry the tools and materials to the site as I've showed you," I advised and the group collected the equipment with glum and morbid anticipation. "Come on," I enthused, "it's not that bad. You might even enjoy it."

They were a motley bunch, one of several teams of volunteers I had taken that day, employed for an hour to perform a practical task. They had already walked eight miles, navigating by map and compass and yet they were late to return to their venue, an adventure training centre near the banks of the Kist. Each group consisted of both men and women, and each group was different. Some keen and willing to get the job done. Some cheerful and enterprising, others flinching and forlorn, and some seemed utterly inept.

We passed various teams of industry as we picked our way through the woods, each group supervised by a Dartmoor Ranger or a Warden of the National Trust, and my new crew followed darkly behind me as we descended a bank. Scoured and rutted by years of water erosion, the steep bridleway was their assignment; to help disperse the watershed by building a series of gutter conduits using cold asphalt chips and lengths of tanalised wood.

To ensure they did the job well, their incentive was to accumulate points for each team challenge, and as wardens of the countryside it was our role as adjudicators to assess their best efforts.

"Friggin slave labour, that's what this is," grumbled Celia, '*Gaggin'forit!*' emblazoned on the t-shirt across her chest. Pallid, tall and skinny, Celia modelled clothes as tardy beans adorn bamboo.

"It's your company training week," I reminded her, "I think they want to see how you cope with unusual tasks."

"So, do you save these jobs each year for us?" enquired Darren, his lip drooping like some pendulous slug.

"We do these kind of jobs all the time," I told him, "mostly in the winter when Dartmoor is quieter."

"Do you enjoy it?" Celia asked incredulously.

"Yes, it's very satisfying creating something people appreciate." But they weren't convinced, and I looked at my wristwatch. "Okay, you have 40 minutes from now to complete the job as described."

Slowly, hesitantly, they assembled themselves into gangs of diggers and makeshift carpenters, mostly the men doing the labouring, whilst the women pondered the three lengths of timber and nails. The men hacking their mattocks at the ground with macho zeal; Darren's lip some agitated mollusc. Celia's hammer hitting wood, dodging an elusive galvanised nail.

"Hit the friggin' thing," Julie told her, her mouth full of gum. But Celia was indignant and dropped the hammer at her feet.

"Go on then, smartarse," she rebuked. "See if you can do better." But Julie discovered she was as dextrous with a hammer as applying lippy to a masticating mule.

A shield bug plotted some deviation through the leaf litter and Karen shrieked, recoiling as it lumbered closer to her perch; the hammer bouncing and resonant. The timber shifting from its moor, emancipated from beneath Karen's ample bottom. And Julie struck her thumb.

"Stupid cow!"

"Darren?" cooed Celia, flaunting her *Gaggin'forit!* B-cups with feminine allure. "Give us a 'and."

Darren, ever hopeful of attracting the opposite sex, extracted his lip, pulled back his shoulders and swaggered proud as Mr cool. Julie was studying him as he approached, jaw chewing emphatically, and her glance switching from eyes, to mouth, to groin.

"Let them sort it," complained Spud, his shirt riding high to reveal a broad expanse of gut. "This is our job, an' that's theirs."

"Bog off, Spud," chided Celia.

"Are you good with yer tool?" smirked Julie and Karen giggled, depressing the wood with her bum. Darren felt his face flush.

"Let them dig, an' we'll knock 'em up," Spud suggested.

"Get lost," said Celia.

"So, Darren," Julie continued unabashed. "Are you going to knock us up, or what?" Darren's lip uncoiling; he was a quivering wreck.

"We could swap over," Spud went on. "What do you reckon, Yogi?"

It took a moment for me to realise he was addressing me, a Ranger figure somewhat detached from their work.

"Yes, why not?" I agreed. Spud was showing some initiative. "But you only have 20 minutes left," I warned.

"Oh, fuck," cursed Celia. "Are we doin' really bad?"

"Yes," I told her bluntly, "you are at the moment." And they were fired into action.

"Spud, get over 'ere and I'll dig," Celia told him. "Julie, shut it an' give us a hand. Karen..?" Celia hesitated, assessing Karen's diminutive and weighty form. "Just park your arse on that wood love while the lads sort it."

Arms sawed, hands nailed while backs bent and grafted over mattocks and spades. No more idle talk. No more innuendo, just a focus allied to getting the job done. Even Karen, more human obelisk than labourer, added her chunky ballast to the task, and with seconds to spare the resultant structure was complete and embedded neatly into the ground.

"Time!" I announced as the last piece of stone was pounded into place and I scribbled silently on my clipboard. Their faces hot from their efforts, their eyes anxious and enquiring.

"Is it alright?" Celia asked, biting her lip with concern. "Sorry we didn't start too good," she apologised.

"For a moment," I told her stoically, "I thought you were the worst group I'd ever met. But you've proved you can work well together when you put your mind to it, *and* you've produced one of the best jobs I've seen."

Their eyes lit up with jubilation. "We did it! We fuckin' did it! Thanks Yogi." And as he left them to find another group, Yogi beamed a smile.

"This is the blunt end..." he began again, "this is the sharp end..."

A Summer Fete

"Bless this summer fete today,
Bless the children who come to play,
Bless the games we have prepared
Bless the food we have to share
So Bless us Lord as we begin
Drizzlewick's annual summer fling."

Everyone cheered. Well, almost everyone save those who had lost their bets.

"Vicar's on form t'day," Arthur grinned.

"First summer ever," George grumbled, parting with a five pound note, and the party balloons were released into the sky as a cloud of helium Doctor Whos.

"Got them at a bargain price," Arthur announced proudly, but it failed to assuage William's pained features. Tight lipped with pique he gazed up at the spectacle, his good eye affixed to the heavens, glass orb listing to abut Miss Pinch's golden squashes.

"Ridiculous bloody things," he growled.

Cradling the swollen pumpkins in her arms, Miss Pinch stopped to swipe a withering glance. "Huh," she retorted huffily. "They're better than your petit pois, any day." And she left him, open mouthed, to retire to the marquee.

"...13:00 hours, the Drizzlewick Dash," drolled Captain Claret on the speaker system, announcing the fete's itinerary with brisk military aplomb. "A cross country run of seven miles... 13:45 is the slippery pole contest... 14:30 hours, best puppy followed by best bitch..."

"*What?*" exclaimed Colonel Brazier beside him.

"Best bitch," Claret repeated laconically, their conversation echoing around the field.

"Ah, that Ranger woman, what's her name?" the Colonel interrupted unaware they were on air. "You know, the Viking heifer with the hair and udders. My God, Claret, she'd put a spark in your musket..."

Abruptly cut off, Captain Claret had discovered the off switch.

Freya became something of a celebrity that day, standing proudly in her Ranger uniform in a corner of the field handing out 'Tread Carefully On Dartmoor' stickers from the back of her Land Rover, or 'Thank You For Taking Moor Care.'

She attracted children and parents and Methuselah parishioners, Freya charming them with posters and Dartmoor pencils, extolling stories of dormice colonies, heron nests and otter holts, or lamenting the decline of the common thrush and water vole.

But it was mostly young men who clamoured as moths to her borealis light, allured by the pheromones she shed by her ambience, her Amazon physique and bewitching smile; Dartmoor's sex icon with pleated hair and walking boots. Indeed, I felt privileged to accompany her, both clad in our pressed khaki shirts, moleskin trousers and waxed leather feet.

"The under 18s are warming up, ready for the Drizzlewick Dash in five minutes. Five minutes for the Drizzlewick Dash!" Captain Claret announced and I glanced over at the starting point where groups of runners prepared themselves for the event, a score of them in the first heat. And Edward was among them, the shortest and the youngest, he was dwarfed by older teenagers, but I knew he was made of sterner stuff.

"So you made it, then," George observed as I bought a beer from the tent.

"Only for a year," I explained, "then I'm back to university. Might do the degree."

"Enjoying it?" Arthur enquired, and I nodded.

"Very much," I admitted. "But I find it very odd to wear a uniform of authority that isn't spat at. I'm amazed how friendly people are and how interested they are to talk to me."

"That's because they don't see you as a threat," Tony spoke up, a fellow incomer who sympathised with our initiation at the Harvest Supper, and I nodded at his sagacity.

"And yet, without the threat, authority would be impotent," I suggested.

"True," he said, "but the trick is how you use it."

It took a while for me to digest his philosophy, my mind full of other things, but as I contemplated the eternal soup of life I considered he was right. Winning hearts and minds was just as vital as the assertiveness of power, the greater balance of which would prove the more effective.

"Come across any crime on the moor, then?" Hyacinth enquired while selling raffle tickets, and I looked at her and shook my head. Although I had been retired for a couple of years now, it seemed her image of me was as some blurred amalgam of a police-Ranger.

"Oh, there's the odd theft from motor vehicle…"

"Do you ever get involved in that?"

"Some of my colleagues have, but it's rare," I smiled at her. "After all, they're Rangers, not policemen."

Happy to assist the police, few Rangers were comfortable dealing with crime, and who could blame them? They did not have the training or the experience. Yet sometimes I found myself visiting remote car parks – popular targets for opportunist thieves - to keep an eye on the world through binoculars, watching for woodpeckers, warblers... and human forms of jackdaw.

We all craned our necks as we studied the skyline, a string of runners ascending the tor. Edward among them, a little blonde head fighting for dominance as the lead group tore away from the rest, scrambling over the crag to disappear from sight.

The spectators were tense, waiting, waiting as the runners ran their course over heath, wood, and vale, to emerge from the field margins. "There they be!" someone affirmed and they jostled for a better view: three dark heads leading, one blonde, hot on their heels as they raced the final mile.

"Come on, Edward," I whispered, torn between handing out leaflets and supporting the hue and cry. It was Freya's turn to get some refreshment from the beer tent, her admirers in tow.

"...and can I have a Dartmoor pencil?" the lady enquired. "They're for my niece," she told me, "she loves Dartmoor..." but I wasn't listening, my mind was with my son, sprinting to the finishing line. "The ponies look so lovely...," and I grabbed stickers and rubbers and pencils and placed them in her hand.

"Here, take these," I told her, then prised a fissure between the expectant crowd.

"Cummon, Al!" someone cried.

"Cummon, Jack!"

"Cummon, Jez!"

"Cummon, Edward!" I yelled. He was neck and neck with number three. Head down; face locked in determination, arms and legs pumping on the final straight. Edward was giving his all.

"Cummon, Edward!" someone else called. It was Lucy.

"Cummon, Edward!" piped David, Anna and John as they wrestled to the front.

"Cummon, Edward!" Freya called out in support and half the crowd looked.

"Cummon, Edward!" they cried.

"Who the 'ell's Edward?" some old farmer asked, and another jabbed his thumb in my direction.

"Ranger's boy."

As the race reached its climax, as the runners stretched for the finishing line, Edward slipped past one, then two to clinch the silver prize.

The greasy pole contest was a great success, the winner being a young Trendlecombe woman who upstaged all contenders by knocking them from the straddled pole to splash into the dammed stream below, her tenure assured by the infamous squeeze of her thighs. And prudently, Colonel Brazier had been evicted from the commentary box to supervise the best vegetable entries.

"The turnips are good this year," the vicar commented, judging a fine root specimen on display.

"The teddies (potatoes) are good an' all," Hyacinth told him.

"My, what a fine crop," he agreed, lovingly fondling the King Edwards. "But I think the rhubarb is quite outstanding."

Colonel Brazier jerked his head. "*What?*" he fired.

"Rhubarb, Colonel!" the vicar repeated, and Brazier glowered at him.

"Bollocks to you too, Vicar!" he volleyed and stormed off to the beer tent.

"He's not having a good day," Hyacinth explained as the vicar looked on open-mouthed.

Our eldest dog, Rosy, was a collie mongrel type whom Lucy entered at the last minute, unprepared, as she urgently arranged Rosy's greying hair with her fingers. Rosy looking at her, appealing for clemency with liquid brown eyes, the only other contestant being a fat old pug that wheezed and farted beneath the judge's examining gaze. But Rosy wore her winning rosette with indifference, Lucy proudly pinning it to her blouse to declare the Best Veteran Bitch.

But it was later, later as the meridian sun declined to its magenta duvet, that inky stellar shawl, the games put away for another year, the stalls dismantled while sleepy girls and sleepy boys receded to their homes.

Then vesper women and vesper men became drawn through the night, possessed by the music that haunted the evening air. Their salivary mouths enticed by the aroma of spit roasted pork rotated and carved for their fare.

Inside the marquee, a bow danced merrily on the violin strings, teasing a tune from its chords. A cello sawed with resonance, a guitar strummed, a banjo twanged, and Miss Pinch's fingers jived the electric keyboard, her magnified eyes blinking in rhythm to some Country and Western ballad.

The dance floor was crowded with local people, Hyacinth and Arthur forming an arch with their arms while the rest danced beneath in pairs, then realigned to do-se-do with a new partner. Wearing less formal clothes, Freya was among them and she had brought Oz, who cavorted with a plump farmer's wife, her rosy cheeks blowing with effort.

The legs pranced, the feet tapped, the hands were swung aloft to briefly join, each participant spinning and bowing in rhythm. Everyone in rhythm, that is, except Colonel Brazier who wobbled and charged his way around the floor as a harried hippopotamus evading a hornet.

"Keep in time, dear!" Mrs Brazier advised as she danced nearby, and his head jerked with the music.

"*What?*"

"Time!"

"10:20!" he declared, deliberating his wristwatch, and collided with William whose glass eye dislodged from its cloister to rocket across the heads of people seated. It struck the amplifier like a meteor, which exploded with a bang, and everyone cowered with fright.

"*Incoming!*" warned Captain Claret, scrambling to his knees to squeeze beneath a table. William stunned and prone upon the floor as his wife groped her way towards him.

"William!" she cried anxiously, and he raised his head. "Arrrgh!" she exclaimed. "Your Willie! Where's your Willie?" And everyone gave her a second glance. "Willie Winky," she explained to their enquiring faces, but they were just as perplexed, indeed, bordering on amusement as they scanned the ground for William's unfortunate detachment.

"I say, old chap..," the Colonel consoled with chagrin, "jolly bad luck."

"His glass eye!" she finally revealed.

"Oh, thank God!" the vicar expounded, his hands clasped in prayer. And everyone sighed with relief.

"It's here!" Miss Pinch announced, plucking the itinerant orb from the smouldering speaker and she raised it up between finger and thumb, examining it invidiously as if it were alive. And his wife took it gratefully. Wiping it with her skirt, she then spat on it before replacing it into her husband's vacant socket.

"There we are, Willie Winky's back where he belongs," she cooed as the fake pupil orbited then descended to her breast. But it bore a scorch mark; some smoky marbled streak that became a distinguishing macula flaw. So never again were ladies alarmed by his leering, forgiving Willie Winky's *amour*. And the band returned to its music-making, one speaker less, but it didn't deter Miss Pinch as she thrashed the keyboard with ragtime jazz.

Emerging stiffly from beneath his table, Captain Claret straightened his tie. Then, swinging his hips to the music he raised a chummy salute to his bumbling colleague.

"Well done, Brazier!" he coughed. "Bloody good show!"

Later, giddy from wine and song, Lucy and I left arm in arm beneath a heavenly sky; music filtering soft and melodious o'er fields of celestial light, the tors as sombre castled walls, shooting stars as cupid arrows impaling lovers to the shadowed clefts and folds. Freya, a reclining silhouette romantic and naked against a silver birch, hair tossed back from her shoulders, mouth parted, eyes hooded; Oz entertaining down under, dining *al fresco* on ambrosial wine.

Sloping away beneath Venus, the river a rippling mantra enchanting a liquid moon, we caressed as the wings of angels to yield to the spell of the night.